THE FALL OF THE HOUSE OF ESCHER
AND OTHER ILLUSIONS

DAVID NIALL WILSON

Contents

Introduction

By Hugh B. Cave

In introducing a first volume of short stories such as this, it seems to be the custom to state that its author is a "new young writer with a future." David Niall Wilson may well be that, but he is also, already, a writer with a voice distinctly his own. I first became aware of this while reading a story of his in a volume of *Year's Best Horror Stories* edited by the late Karl Edward Wagner, whose judgment I deeply respected.

That story, "A Candle Lit in Sunlight," is one of those in the book you now hold in your hands. As well it should be.

"A Candle Lit in Sunlight" struck me at once as being the work of a writer with a solid, deep-searching style and an unusually active imagination. Put more simply, it is the kind of story you don't come across every week, month, or even year. Mary Magdalene a creature of the night? No run-of-the-mill writer would come up with such an idea, let alone be able to weave a gripping story around it and make you believe it might really have happened

Yet "Candle" is not even my favorite in this collection of Wilson's stories. Very much at home with religious themes, the author has included two others here, "On the Road to Damascus" and "On the Third Day," that rival it in excellence. Like everything else here, these are presented in depth, with their players coming through as living, thinking, feeling people—a rather radical departure from much of today's new fiction in which characters are little more than names racing through violent action and uttering four-letter words at every opportunity. To my way of thinking, "On the Third Day" is a genuine classic. I have been a writer for some sixty years and a reader for longer than that, and consider this one of the most powerful tales I have ever encountered.

It would seem that there is also a touch of Poe and H. P. Lovecraft in David Niall Wilson. "The Fall of the House of Escher" brings to mind both of them, and not merely because of its title. This particular tale, it seems to me, is not so much a rewrite of Poe's "Fall of the House of Usher" as an updated companion piece, if you will. You see the frightening house in Wilson's story. You smell it, hear it, feel it. You know it's alive and find yourself wandering about in it, wondering fearfully what's going to happen to you next.

In "Yours, the Vengeance," you learn that author Wilson also has some firmly entrenched ideas about the planet we live on and those greedy souls who would despoil it. A strange little story is this, now whispering along in a kind of fairy-tale magic, now shudderingly grim and ghastly. And then you read a story like "Sparkling Eyes" and realize that author Wilson is a man of widely differing moods, for here is a tender probing of the mind of a man in love. A love story in a volume such as this?

INTRODUCTION

Yes. Despite its intricate seascape of color, mood, and killer whales, that's what this one is.

David Niall Wilson edited an excellent small press magazine called *The Tome* for over eight years, in which he presented some fine fiction by other writers. This little volume is proof that he, himself, is a writer very much to be reckoned with.

The Fall of the House of Escher

When my friend's home first came into sight, I let the car coast to a stop, not quite ready to turn the corner; unable to make that final commitment. There were a lot of memories tied up in that old place, good, bad, and indelible. Lessons had been learned there—pounded home. That was the past.

The present was an almost impossible to conceive reversal of fortunes—the abused, mal-adjusted young man as heir, the family mansion his home, not his prison. My mind couldn't quite press the pieces into place. I still expected, once I pulled into that drive and parked, that Old Man Hector would slam open the door, glaring at me with those crazed, impossibly large eyes, and demand to know what I wanted—why I wouldn't leave his son alone.

Johnny would be peeking, as always, around the side of his father's leg, his own eyes begging me not to run, to come in and, if only for a little while, to rescue him from his prison.

I could remember several times that Johnny had borne the signs of his father's displeasure, black and yellowish bruises beneath his eyes. Deep lacerations poorly healed on his arms. Fingers with nails blackened from being slammed in doors or windows. He never spoke about them, these battle-scars of his adolescence, but without speech we understood one another better than most people could in years of conversation.

He shared one trait with his father—the eyes. Old Man Hector's, as I said, were huge and frightening. Johnny's were deep, haunted, and full of a desperate pain that cried for release.

Again, that was the past. I took my foot off the brake and let the car glide forward once again, rounding the corner and nosing it between the gates that led to the Hector homestead. I noted as I passed that the place had a much more dilapidated look about it. Apparently Johnny hadn't inherited his father's love of the immaculate.

I would be at a loss to put into words how the sight of that place affected me. It was nothing so much as a sensation—an aura of "wrongness," that emanated from its walls and glared out at me through the dusty, empty eyes of its windows. Straightening my shoulders and driving on, I tried to put the notion from my head. It was only the past again, I thought, weaving its way into the fabric of the present, trying to disrupt the design.

That was Johnny talking. Even as a boy he had been obsessed with designs, patterns of all kinds. "Everything has a pattern, Kyle," he told me once. "Everything."

If that was true, then there was something deeply troubling about the pattern of that old house, something left over from its previous master, I suppose. As curious as I was to see my old friend again, to see what life had done with him, I was in no hurry to enter that shadowy den of childhood nightmares.

I parked near the front, noting the absence of any other vehicles with a slight frown. If it hadn't been for the short letter tucked into my jacket pocket, penned in Johnny's unmistakable scrawling style, I'd have thought the place deserted. I certainly wouldn't have stayed there, given the choice.

The front door banged open as I stepped from my car, and past and present snapped together like the pulled ends of a time warp rubber band. He was the same, and yet, not. The eyes hadn't changed at all, nor had the wild, waving locks of hair that framed his gaunt face, unless it was to grow longer and even less controlled. He was taller, yes, and the emaciated, almost surreal thinness of his frame was accentuated by the new height. He was a haunted scarecrow with a crooked smile, and I felt the years between us slipping away as I stepped forward to take the hand he offered. I wondered briefly what impression I had made, how he would perceive the product of our years apart, but only briefly.

"Johnny?"

"Of course, Kyle, who else would I be?"

Those words broke down the final barriers. They were so—Johnnyesque. Suddenly it was as though we had not been apart, as though I'd seen him only days, or hours before. I released his hand, stepping forward to give him a quick hug. I hadn't been aware, until that moment, just how much I'd actually missed him.

"I'm glad you came," he said simply. "I have things to show you, things nobody else would understand. I have to show someone…"

And that was that. We took my bags inside, tossed them quickly into one of the many empty bedrooms on the upper floor of the old place, and headed for what had once been his father's den. A sense of déjà vu hit me then with staggering force. The den, forbidden territory—the fear was tangible, even with Old Man Hector's wrath a dead and empty threat. I watched Johnny's eyes for signs of it, any indication that he felt the odd, emotional impulses that were assaulting my senses, but his expression never changed.

He pushed the door open without a thought and gestured for me to enter, his face alight with an eagerness I recognized instantly. Johnny had lived a childhood of obsessions, strung one after the next, and with each ensuing thought or idea came the overwhelming desire to share.

It was this desire that filled his eyes at that moment, and I felt a thrill of expectation as I slipped through the door ahead of him. He had had some crazy ideas, but all memorable. His plans and experiments failed as often as not, but their magic had always been in their presentation.

"I've been working on this for a long time," he began, following me into the room and taking one of two chairs that flanked an old, water-stained mahogany table. I had a fleeting desire to wipe it off; it was a beautiful old piece, but I ignored it. Johnny was not one to care about material things. To him, I'm sure, it was a table, nothing more. On its surface sat two empty glasses and a half full decanter of bourbon.

He poured two hefty shots of the liquor, smiling shyly as he did so. "It was father's," he said reverently, the first mention of his deceased sire, "but now it's mine."

He sat down across from me, took a quick gulp from the glass, and continued. "It started with the stories," he said quickly, "the ones in father's old books. At first, when he was gone, the house seemed so—empty. I spent a lot of time in his library, reading things I'd never been allowed to touch. I learned a lot, and it got me to thinking, you know?"

I did, and once something got him "to thinking," it could lead to hours, days, even months of obsessive experimentation and study. I remembered the library, as well. It was a huge room, right next door to where we sat.

We'd been allowed in there once or twice as children, but only when Old Man Hector had gotten it into his head to share some bit of "learning" with us.

He continued. "I had never really understood how much there was to read, how much there was to know. I was reading a story by Edgar Allen Poe—you've heard of him?"

I laughed at that, though more out of amazement at my friends sheltered naiveté than at his question. Sometimes I forgot that he'd been schooled at home, that his life had not been that of a normal boy. "Yes," I replied, "I had to read him in high school, but that was years ago."

Ignoring my laughter, he nodded his satisfaction with my answer and went on. "It was a story called "The Fall of the House of Usher" that started it all. The words were so descriptive, so… precise. He wrote of places, configurations of inanimate objects—even certain specific "spaces" in existence that for some reason affect your mind. I'd never really thought about it before then, but I realized at once that he was right."

Now my curiosity was peaked. What he was speaking of was one and the same as the odd emotional reaction I had experienced upon seeing his house, and again upon entering the room in which we sat. But where would it lead, I wondered.

"That was just a story, Johnny," I said, knowing I was fueling the fires. "Poe wrote fiction."

He made a waving gesture, as though brushing away an annoying insect, and continued. "It isn't the story, Kyle, but the concept! Poe was a writer, a sensitive. He wouldn't have been able to write so vividly about something unless he was familiar with it, unless he'd felt it.

"I started searching. I read other authors, Machen, Blackmoor, Stoker, Lovecraft; my father had a rather extensive collection of this sort of thing. I found the same type of references in all of them, particularly in the Lovecraft. His work almost screams of knowledge just beyond his grasp—of sensations he could not quite explain."

My friend's eyes were growing wilder, and I began to be concerned. I'd seen him excited like this before, but there was a barely leashed fanaticism in the intensity of his gaze that itched at my senses.

"Are you saying," I asked him, forming my words carefully, "that these authors saw something other people did not?"

"No," he answered immediately, "of course not. I'm saying that they could "sense" things that others couldn't, or at least they had the ability to transform those sensations into words that would convey the sensation to others less sensitive than themselves.

"That's why I had to go beyond them."

He took another slug of the bourbon then, sitting back and looking at me as if awaiting some particular response. I didn't know exactly what to say.

"You went beyond them," I repeated blindly. "You mean you wrote more or better stories?"

His eyes flickered with a momentary emotion, either disappointment or frustration, I couldn't be certain, and he sighed. "The stories aren't the point, Kyle, I said that already. It's the concept, the idea that inanimate objects in particular patterns can cause—effects."

He must have been aware of how vague this sounded, because he threw back the last of his drink in exasperation and fell silent for a moment, deep in thought. I got the distinct impression that his mind, which operated at speeds and in dimensions all its own, was busy trying to translate his "great concept" into common idiot terms so he could get on with his lecture. I can't explain it, but it felt good to see him that way, a fond memory come back to life. I had always dragged like an anchor when he was on a philosophical roll.

The silence that surrounded us was less benevolent, however. The insidious chill that had assaulted me upon entering the room returned, and I began to glance nervously about the room. The shadows were deep and elongated, cowing the dim light of the one lamp easily as the day faded toward evening. Dust and cobwebs coated everything, here and there desecrated by an occasional footprint or smudge, but for the most part reinforcing my earlier impression of abandonment.

Just as I was about to break the silence myself, to question him about his father, and what he was doing with himself, Johnny's eyes flashed up to grab mine.

"There are things I want to show you," he said slowly, "things I want you to understand, but they cannot be met lightly. I have come to my conclusions over long hours of research and study; I have come to them prepared."

Something in his manner of speech drilled the icicle spikes of fear deeper into my spine. Rather than familiar, his odd, disheveled appearance and bright, haunted eyes began to blend in with our eerie surroundings, giving him an aspect of warped surreality. I got a sudden flash of Johnny's father's face, superimposed over his own, and I began to feel some of the awe and fear I'd felt as a child returning.

"I'm not sure I understand what you're getting at," I said, glancing at the dust encrusted window, up to the grimy glitter of the ancient crystal chandelier, anywhere but back into those eyes.

"I'm quite certain that you do not understand," he snapped peevishly. "That is the problem, Kyle. You need to understand the basis of what I will show you—for your own safety."

Now I was beyond nervous. His attitude and the looming, dismal aura of that room and the building surrounding it were becoming more than I could bear. I turned to him, but he was already on his feet, standing so close at my side that I nearly jumped from my seat at the sudden sight of him. He loomed over me like a giant, grotesque insect, bending so that his face was right up to mine—so near that I could feel his breath on my skin, moist and chill.

"Come," he said quickly. "I will show you what followed the stories; maybe that will help. You must hurry, though, it's getting dark, and the light has to be just right…"

I wasn't sure that I wanted to see what had followed the stories, but I was absolutely certain that I'd had enough of that room, so I rose and followed. He must have mistaken my relief at leaving the influence of that depressing place for enthusiasm, because his eyes brightened perceptibly as I followed him down the hall and into the next room.

I stopped immediately inside the door, staring about myself in wonder. The walls were completely covered in paintings, prints, and sketches. The frames were fitted so closely together that it gave the impression of one colossal collage. That alone was enough to disconcert me, but the contents of the frames were even more disturbing.

I recognized much of the work, Bosch, Dali, and predominantly—Escher. There were melting clocks and birds that blended with fish and back to birds, there were stairways that diverged at impossible angles and bent back in upon themselves, hallways that continued in endless progression into tiny, infinitesimal dots of ink—and more, much more than my mind could reconcile all at once. The effect was staggering.

I stumbled backward, falling painfully against the frame of the doorway. My head was spinning with a sudden twist of vertigo, and my thoughts were choppy and inconsistent, like a stuttering projector trying to pass a reel of film.

I felt Johnny's hands on my shoulders, trying and failing to hold me upright. I couldn't rid myself of the images from those pictures, strobing through my consciousness, overlaying my normal field of vision and denying my mind escape.

David Niall Wilson

The nausea that overcame me then was overpowering. My stomach heaved, trying to physically void what my mind rejected, a poison as sure and powerful as strychnine. It was an instinctive reaction, and somehow it must have worked, for the next coherent thoughts I can remember were that I was on my knees, and that my stomach ached horribly. Every muscle in my body was taut, stretched beyond the normal limits of tension. I raised my head, staring about myself with bleary eyes, and there was Johnny.

He was standing over me, wringing his hands in dismay, but there was a strange, expectant gleam in his eyes at the same time. I shuddered again as his gaze brought back the memory of what had come before.

I closed my eyes for just a moment, clearing my thoughts, and then stumbled to my feet, bracing myself against the wall of the hallway. Somehow we had left that room—that nightmare. I shook my head in confusion.

"What happened?" I asked, rubbing the back of my head where it had hit the door frame when I fell. "How the hell did we get out here, and what did that damned room do to me, Johnny?"

"You saw," he stated cryptically. "Come on, let's get you something to drink, and I'll try again to explain. There is so much to know, to understand, I..." He clamped his mouth shut and spun on his heel, hurrying off down the hall. I followed as quickly as I could, wondering just how I was going to get myself the hell out of that place before any more "revelations" befell me.

I caught up with him in doorway to the kitchen, where he met me holding out a glass with a few ice cubes in it and some water. "Don't have any aspirin, do you?" I asked, rubbing my head again. There was a good-sized knot forming on the back of my scalp, throbbing thunderously in counterpoint to the beat

12

of my heart. He just looked at me, as though incapable of understanding my concern over my headache in the face of his "revelations."

"There may be some upstairs in the medicine chest," he said at last. "I'll go and check."

I wandered back into the hallway, glancing at the old portraits on the walls and the dry, peeling wallpaper. It was more like a ruin than a home, and the sense of decay was overpowering. Odors invaded my nostrils that I could not understand having overlooked before that moment. Shadows melted from the edges and the corners and the flickering, yellow light of the old lamps cowered in the face of the groping fingers of darkness.

I backed away from one wall, the ghost touch of eyes boring through my back spurring me onward, only to be confronted by a portrait on the opposite wall that sent me reeling confusedly back again. It was Old Man Hector, eyes wider even than I remembered, and crazier. Those eyes followed me as I turned, nearly bumping into Johnny, who appeared from the stairs.

"What is it?" he asked. His voice did not sound concerned. Again I felt an undercurrent of excitement, of anticipation. I'd had about enough.

"It's this damned house," I answered, my voice cracking from the strain, "and I think you know it. It's like there are eyes in the walls, watching. It feels just like it did being in the cellar with your father upstairs, wondering every minute if he'd bust in on us, foaming at the mouth and crazy. What the hell are you doing here, Johnny? This place isn't... right."

He clapped his hands, a little exclamation of what might have passed for delight escaping his lips. I thought for a second that he might dance about in a circle, and the mental image this thought conjured was just enough to break the solemnity of the moment. He didn't offer me an answer, but he did offer two large aspirin tablets, which I accepted and gulped gratefully, washing them down with the last of the water.

"You felt it again," he said. "The aura. I must be getting close; we're not even in the room!"

I didn't bother to ask him what the hell he was talking about this time. I was half convinced that my old friend was as loony as a Jay Bird, and the other half convinced that I was as well. It was only an old house, after all. All his bullshit about "auras" and inanimate patterns was beginning to seep through into my mind.

His attitude changed abruptly. "Let's go into the front room," he said solicitously. "You look as though you should sit down for a while, and I could use another glass of that bourbon. We still have a lot of catching up to do."

I nodded, not really trusting his new, glib manner, but agreeing wholeheartedly with both sitting and drinking. The front room, while it had not been as forbidden as the den, was another hazy spot in my memory.

As we entered, I saw that the ancient Victrola had been replaced by the first sign of truly modern life I'd seen to that point; a large, expensive-looking component stereo system. There were tape cases and album covers strung haphazardly about the floor at its feet, like offerings before an idol, and several microphones hung about it from stands and precarious perches of all sorts.

"When did you become a music lover?" I asked as he returned with the bottle and the two glasses.

He poured the drinks, a huge grin splitting his face. "I always wanted to listen to the music—you know that. Papa punished me many times for hiding here, lying under a couch or crouched under a table, while he played his records. It had such power, that sound. I always felt transported, as though everything here was a dream, and the key to escaping it was the sound. I had to buy this when I was finished with the paintings, you see. The next step was the sound."

The gleam was back in his eyes, and I had the inexplicable urge to rise and bolt from the room. I felt like a fly, caught unaware by a grinning spider; all I could do was to sit there dumbly and to listen as he once again began to spout his madness.

"I don't know how I could have missed it at the first. It's so obvious, don't you think?" My blank stare brought the closest to an expression of anger to his face that I had ever seen. It brought out his father's features again, and the chill returned tenfold to the nerve endings in my spine.

"Really, Kyle," he berated me softly, handing over one of the glasses of bourbon, "you really must start paying attention. The music, Kyle, it can affect us even more strongly than the stories, or the pictures. It reaches further into your physical form and your ethereal being all at once. It can bring tears, or joy, or sorrow, and all that is necessary is sound."

He moved to the stereo, and before I could voice my unease, he had pushed the play button and the tape deck snapped into life. A loud hiss filled the speakers as the leader ran past the play heads, and again I considered flight. He was crazy; there was no need for me to remain any longer to figure that out. I had actually tensed my muscles to rise when the first sound erupted from the stereo, pinioning me as neatly as any struggling insect in a cigar box.

At first it was music, or bits and pieces of music. There were low, thrumming chords, bass strings reverberating so deeply and powerfully that the room about them seemed to shimmer, vibrating in the grasp of the booming notes. Then the sound evolved. It twisted in upon itself and back out again, high pitched screeches, rending groans, all vibrant, all loud—too loud.

I felt the glass shake in my hand and forced myself to toss off the rest of the drink. The glass fell to the floor, the sound of its shattering lost in the hypnotic rhythm of the stereo's blast. Specters flitted about the perimeters of my sight, peripheral variations in the room that moments earlier had seemed stable—solid and constant.

Johnny sat through it all, oblivious, eyes riveted on mine. His features, like the walls, melted and morphed constantly. One moment I saw my childhood friend, face frozen in concentration, the next I saw his father—Old Man Hector— cackling and grinning madly. There were other faces. Some pushed into the walls from the inside, like fetuses pressed against the skin of the womb in an ultrasound from hell.

I screamed. It was a silent meaningless act of futility, swept away and lost in the madness of the relentless flood of sound from the stereo. My scream molded itself into the fabric of the moment, pressed itself into indentured servitude to the "music" of Johnny's waking nightmare house.

Then it was over. Just like that. No sound but the hiss of the tape deck, run out of footage, and heavy rasping sounds I finally identified as my own breath. Johnny had risen—when had he done that?—and was rewinding the tape. His features showed no sign of the intensity of the experience I'd just endured. They were stoic, detached.

"I..." words would not pop free of my mouth. My breath, though taken in heaving gasps, was inadequate to satisfy my lungs. I closed my eyes, fighting for control, and managed to choke out a few wheezing sounds. "What... what did you do? The sound—the walls—I..." A wave of sickening dizziness washed through me, doubling me over with sudden nausea.

Johnny moved to my side, a hand on my shoulder. When I looked up, his eyes held no compassion. "It was the next step," he said simply. "After the stories, the pictures. After the pictures, the sound. Now you begin, I think, to see."

"I see that you're losing your mind," I snapped, gaining a bit more control of my senses. "What did you do to me with that tape? Those pictures? This whole house is—wrong— Johnny, can't you see that?"

Johnny's eyes sparkled. "Of course I see it, Kyle," he said, seating himself again and refilling his own bourbon glass, which he handed over to his friend. "I saw it when we were young, but I didn't see it, you know? It took solitude, and that story, to piece it together for me. So many pieces—like a great puzzle. I have to know where it all leads."

"Well," I answered slowly, pouring the bourbon straight down my throat without even a pause to swallow. "I know where it's leading me. I'm getting out of here, Johnny, and I think you should come with me."

Johnny's face went blank. His eyes glazed, then became dull mirrors, reflecting unbelief. "How can you?" he asked at last, pouring yet another glass of the bourbon and sipping it himself before handing it over. "How can you see so much, and not want to know the rest?"

"Jesus, Johnny," I burst out, taking the proffered glass and, ignoring the quickly mounting buzz from the liquor, "it's not right for Christ's sake. When something feels wrong, you don't take it a bit further so you can study it; you turn around and go the other damned direction! Those pictures, that tape..." I shuddered, holding the glass out to be filled once again. "I've never felt like that. Even when your father was here, it was never like that.

"There were faces, Johnny. Did you see the faces, too? They were pressing out of the walls, rippling over the ceiling. Your

17

face changed—for a minute I thought you were your father. No way was it all the sound from that tape. It's this damned house, and I'm getting out of it."

"You should at least stay the night." Johnny said, changing his tack as smoothly as if they'd been discussing the weather. "You've had quite a bit to drink, and that bump on your head is half the size of an apple. You shouldn't drive like that. If you don't want to share my creations…" there was a break in his voice at this point, a sliver of a crack that ran through the emotionless veneer of his face, but then it was gone.

At the mention of the drinks, I suddenly felt the heaviness in my eyelids, and the throbbing pain in my head became more noticeable. Shit, I thought miserably, reaching up to rub the lump on my head gingerly, he's right.

The thought of spending an entire night in that creepy old home nearly froze my blood, but, after all, that had been the original plan, hadn't it? At what point had this place—this visit—become the enemy? Maybe I hit my head harder than I thought, I mused.

"You're right," I said at last. "I'm pretty tired, actually. Maybe things will seem different in the morning." I rose shakily to my feet, and Johnny reached out a hand to steady me.

"One thing, though," I said, catching my friends eyes with my own (was that gloating I saw?), "no more tapes, okay? I think I've experienced about all I can handle in a single day."

Johnny nodded (too quickly?) and led him back to the front of the old house, and to the stairs that led to the upstairs bedrooms. "I have some work to finish up," he said. "I'll see you in the morning, and we'll discuss everything."

I was in no mood for thoughts of discussion or anything else but sleep. "Right," I mumbled, stumbling up the stairs into the gloom. "See you in the morning."

"In the morning," Johnny echoed, staring after me until I disappeared from his sight.

I'm not sure if it was the sound that awakened me, or the undulating, side to side motion of the bed. Shaking the cobwebs from my brain as quickly as I could, I pushed back the blankets and peered into the darkness.

The room was pitch black. There should have been some light, some form of illumination, but there was not. My heart iced over as, once again, the bed shifted with a sinuous surge. The room vibrated with heavy, reverberating crashes. A flash of terror flickered through me at the sound (but it wasn't precisely the sound was it?) The air was alive with sensations that prickled along the hairs of my arm and down my spine.

I'd experienced the weight of unseen eyes on my consciousness before, but now the eyes bored in from every direction, from above, below, unrelenting pressure that fluctuated with the rippling of the bed beneath me. I cowered against the headboard, unwilling to swing my legs over the side of the bed and rise, yet repulsed by the odd reptilian life that seemed to have possessed it.

It was then that I distinguished the first scream amid the pounding, reverberating thunder; a high pitched, petrified wail that clawed at my ears for attention. Despite my own fear, I couldn't clear the new image that rose unbidden to my mind. Johnny; Johnny in trouble; Johnny in deep.

I shuddered, closing my eyes and reaching up to press my palms against my ears, but it was too late.

"Damn you Johnny!" I screamed the words into the void, letting the fear and the anger that filled me burst free in one huge ripping burst. "Damn you and your house to hell!"

I flipped back the blanket and leapt from the bed, avoiding the rippling touch of the bed as I sprang to where I knew the dresser must be. It was. I couldn't make it out, but my groping hands managed to close around the cool solid surface of the wood. I walked my fingers over it until they found my pants, and I yanked them free, pulling them on in one fluid motion. Fear motivated me, but it no longer controlled my movements. Not until I heard the second scream.

The sound that grated through the walls and imbedded itself in my brain was the voice of insanity, the cry of an anguished soul. Somewhere in its depths I recognized the remnant of my friend.

I stumbled forward, tripping over my boots and slamming into the wall. I knelt there, stunned, for a long moment, and then pulled the boots on and rose again, feeling my way down the wall toward the door.

I was nearly there when the first face pushed itself free of the paneled surface and gummed my hand blindly, a sucking, mindless sound erupting from the contact. Crying out I pulled free, spinning along the wall and tripping out in to the hall, where the blackness finally gave way to an odd, greenish glow. It radiated from the stairs—from below. The screams rent the heavy, shadowy air once more, and the force of them, a physical wrench at my mind sent me reeling forward.

I took the hall as quickly as I could, fighting for my balance as the floor, grown treacherous, shifted subtly beneath my pounding feet. Nearly missing the first step, I stumbled headlong into the madness I knew awaited me below. I don't know how I knew, but on some primal level, I did.

The next level, I thought. He's found his damnable "next level".

The stairs seemed to fight me, tilting to send me crashing against the walls and then back. The rails along the far side elongated and melted, leaving holes through which I might plunge if I failed to maintain a tight enough grip on their oily, slithering surface. I clawed my way downward, wading into the green glow.

There were forms swirling about in the haze, faces flitting through my line of sight, but I ignored them, forcing my eyes to remain focused on the hall — or what had been the hall — ahead of me. The walls were not there, or if they were, they were so enmeshed in the green haze and the flickering images that I couldn't discern them. Somehow the strip of colored carpet that ran down the center of the hall was still there.

Though I couldn't tell how far I'd moved, I could make out darker oblongs in the green shadows, cavernous mouths that I knew must be the doors to the rooms. I passed the door that I knew to be the den and its access to the library. The source of the glowing light seemed to be further down the hall, and I waded through the clinging morass toward the next door, the room that held the paintings.

"What the hell have you done now, Johnny?" I panted, fighting to keep my breath steady. "What in hell is going on?"

I felt a tightening in my chest as I remembered the sensation my first glimpse of that room had brought about. Steeling my nerves against the fear, I reached for the framework of the door. It shifted beneath my grip, and I felt wet, slick ropes of — something — slide over my fingertips, lingering on my forearms as I slipped through the opening. The wood rippled again — was it acknowledging my presence? It moved toward me, like a snake coiling to strike, but I was through, shooting into the room beyond and staggering in a slow circle, searching, looking for my friend.

There were no frames hanging from the walls, not any longer. The images — fish, crucified bodies, bird creatures climbing from huge, orange-colored cracked eggs to cavort with demon things that staggered about on fantastically exaggerated limbs—all of it had melted together into a whirling nightmare world, interacting and moving.

I spun quickly, staying as far from the treacherous surface of the walls as possible. I cringed back as one of the huge, obscene faces mashed itself out through the now pliant surface of the room to mewl at me, deadened tongue.

"Johnny!" I screamed, but the sound was lost... impotent.

One of the bird creatures, a Bosch creation of grotesquely elongated legs and staring, alien eyes, turned its attention on me. Somehow the creature was looking through from that other world hell and locking its eyes with mine.

It let out a terrible screech, and suddenly the images all turned, focusing on my back pedaling form. Squawks, grunts, hisses, cries, all of these sounds and more rose as the creatures of the paintings spun on me, rippling along the wall in waves that pushed outward from the surface of the wall to flow inexorably toward me.

Diving through the doorway into the greenish haze of the outer hall, I felt my heart hammering painfully in his chest. My breath was becoming more labored. The greenish air was not quite the air of my world—not enough oxygen. I moved farther down the hall.

There was one more opening, one room Johnny hadn't taken me into, and it was from there that I heard the screams again, weaker and more hopeless, crying to my soul.

It was also the source of the greenish light. I waded forward, cursing and swinging my arms to clear a space in front of my face. The nearer I came to the doorway, the harder it was to breathe—and the brighter the glow became. It was like one of those luminous toys they hand out on Halloween, the kind you snap in the center to make them glow, but I was wading through it.

Every movement was in slow motion. Instead of just my feet touching the floor, every inch of my body interacted with the surrounding—air? My head pounded with sounds beyond my experience, sounds that evoked images—emotions. I alternately cried, cursed, screamed, and laughed. Through it all, I clung tenaciously to the one sound I recognized, fought through the haze toward the center of the room. Over and over, though it was weakening, the pathetic sound of a man screaming—Johnny screaming—reached out to me.

"Johnny!" I screamed and ducked to the side as one of the huge, demented faces rose from the floor beneath me, swiping at me blindly with its grotesque tongue. The air was clearing as I neared the center of the room. The green light was painfully intense, but the haze was receding. Or maybe I was just passing into the next stage—of what? Hell?

"Johnny!" I screamed again. I could hear him more clearly, but there was no answer to my call, only the screams, heart wrenching, hopeless screams.

Then I saw it. I knew he must be in the center of the room, and I knew—at last—what it was that Johnny had wanted to show me. Beyond the stories, beyond the pictures, and the sound—Jesus. He'd brought the images to life, blended the paintings, the sound, all of it—with the house!

There were three separate sculptures rising from the floor, constructed of metal and wood and plastic, some obviously garbage, others of more obscure origin. The first was a twisted mesh work of animal forms, and human bodies sculpted of razor wire and wrought iron that melted together, then sprang apart—a maelstrom of Escheresque images in 3-D.

The second was similar to the first, though less harsh, more fluid. It seemed to be the source of the greenish light—glittering with a green metal sheen that was painful to the sight. Neither of these drew my attention.

It was the center of the room that riveted my feet in place, that stole the last of my labored breath, just when I needed it to scream and scream and scream until I could blank it all from my mind.

It was a staircase, or several staircases. They bent and arched and twisted, seeming to melt and to disappear at odd angles into the air. I couldn't understand how it stood—what held it in place—where the tips of the stairways disappeared to? But even the bizarre impossibility of the structure—the real-world impossibility of Escher in three dimensions—or more?—could not distract me from Johnny.

On the center stair—three quarters of the way up—Johnny's hands, clutching like clawed talons, scrabbled on the steps. His legs, disappearing upward into—nothing?—extended beyond the top of the stair; but they were not there! Johnny Hector's torso protruded from the nothingness above the stair, and it was obvious that something—in there?—was pulling on him, claiming him.

His mouth moved in a constant flow of screams, shuddering intakes of breath, and more screams. His eyes, those huge, soulful eyes, were opened so widely that the flesh around them seemed stretched—warped.

They locked on mine. A slight flicker of recognition transited their surface, and then was gone. They were empty—empty of all save pain, eyes that had seen hell and couldn't erase the image.

I tried to move forward, to reach out for my friend's hand, but just as my groping fingers stretched forth to entwine themselves with Johnny's, the stair gave a mighty lurch, rippling up and away from me like the coils of some bizarre serpent, and my friends clawing grip was ripped free.

I stared up in horror as Johnny made one last desperate effort, heaving himself back down the stairway, one foot, another. Old, gnarled hands appeared, gripping his ankles, and then with a sharp convulsive kick he was free.

I saw a face then, pressing out against the nothingness and framed by the aura of the green light from the other sculpture, and I screamed again. I knew that face. It had hounded me through my nightmares for years.

"What are you doing here, boy?" The voice was huge, booming. It had no direction, rising from all sides at once. "What are you doing in my room?"

Johnny was backed against the whipping form of the stairs, his hands white-knuckled as he clung for purchase. He was cowered back as far as humanly possible, as if he could press himself through the sinuous conglomeration of metal and wood... as if he could hide.

I staggered to my feet, lurching forward, but it was too late. The stairway rolled back into itself, spinning and contracting, and with a final screech of horror and dismay, Johnny was sucked into nothingness, drawn inward to some indescribable vacuum. Gone.

The next moment lasted an eternity. The sound ceased. It didn't taper off, nor did it fade or change. It was just not there. Nothing. Silence. Reality snapped into place so suddenly and completely, that my eyes were momentarily blinded by the disorienting twist that removed it all. Like Johnny, gone.

The first two statues stood, twisted and ugly, but the stairs were gone. There wasn't even a mark on the floor to indicate where they had stood. As far as the world that now surrounded me was concerned, they had never existed.

I felt a shiver begin in my legs, progress to a tremble, and then I was quaking, barely able to stand. I collapsed painfully to my knees, eyes still locked on the empty space before me.

Hours later, when the heaving, shuddering sobs had ceased, when I remembered where I was and who I was, I rose. My legs were cramped and knotted but I forced them into motion, gaining momentum. I passed through the hall swiftly and up the stairs. Without a pause I grabbed my bags, my keys, and was back in the hall—back down the stairs, and out the door, out into the cool darkness of the night beyond.

I stopped by the door of my car, breathing in the freshness of the air, staring into the endless normality of the starry sky. As I opened the door and climbed inside, I shivered once again. Was it endless normality? Would I ever believe that again?

I drove off into the darkness, consciously striving not to twitch as I watched for faces, pressing themselves from the depths of the sky.

A Candle Lit in Sunlight

Lucifer watched with deep interest, and some concern, the arrival of The Christ upon the Earth. Well aware that he could not prevent it, and unwilling to forego the amusement, in any case, he set about sowing the seeds of jealousy, fear, and distrust that would later lead to the crucifixion. Once satisfied, he waited for the child to grow. A small mountain of dead children grew on Christ's birthday, sacrificed by those who feared the birth of a king.

Men seem often given to strange excesses in the solving, or prevention, of problems. I saw it as a shame; Lucifer saw the destruction not at all. His eyes were turned Heavenward in search of a glimpse of the anger he knew his actions would spark. I walked the Earth in his shadow, watching. In the Christ, he saw another part of his enemy, another work to corrupt. I saw beauty, a piece of something forever lost to me. Lucifer saw none of that; his hate had become too great. I saw him as he was, and I loved him. The Christ was very beautiful.

{From the Book of the Gospel, According to Judas Iscariot} Judas 1:1

1 And it came to pass that Jesus went alone into the desert to be tempted of the devil. 2 He remained there forty days and forty nights, fasting, and on the fortieth night, he hungered. 3 The tempter came before him then, asking, "If you are truly the son of God, turn these stones to loaves of bread" 4 Jesus answered him, "It is written: 'man does not live on bread alone, but on every word that comes from the mouth of God.'"

5 Then the tempter led him to the highest point of the temple. 6 "If you are truly the son of God, cast yourself down, for it is written:

'He will command his angels

concerning you,

And they will lift you up in their

hands,

So that you will not strike your foot against stone.'"

7 Jesus answered, "It is also written, 'do not put the Lord your God to the test.'"

8 The devil took him to a very high mountain and showed him all of the kingdoms of the world in their splendor. 9 "Bow down and worship me," he said, "and I will give them all to you."

10 Jesus replied, "Away from me, Satan, for it is written, 'Worship the Lord your God, and serve him only.'"

11 The devil laughed and gestured, raising from the sands a temptress. 12 "See here the things craved by man," he said, waving his arm to include the cities below. 13 "You are Son of man, does she not please you?"

14 And Jesus, seeing that she was fallen from Heaven, and sorely used, beckoned to the temptress, saying, "For all who would follow me, there burns a light in my father's house."

15 And the temptress fell to her knees, forsaking the devil and his darkness. 16 In an awful rage, Lucifer laid upon her a curse, bringing a great thirst which could be sated only by the lifeblood of man, and saying, "Feast you upon the fruits of his labor, for I say unto you, you shall be his undoing." 16 Then the devil left them, and angels came and attended Jesus. 17 Fleeing into the desert, the temptress wept.

I hid for many days among the burning sands, and the thirst grew, grasping at my thoughts and twisting them beyond my control. I heard echoing laughter in the pits below, but had no concentration to spare it. As the sun dipped a final time, on the eighth day, I came to the fringes of the city of Galilee. At that time, the horror of what had befallen me was not clear in my mind. I slipped through the shadows of the city as a silent mist, searching for that which could end the thirst, hungering for freedom to follow him who had promised me hope.

———

Isabella, late in returning to her home from that of her sister, Jessamine, stopped at the sound of footsteps in the night. No direction lay in the sound. It seemed to echo from every shadow. When her steps ceased, the others ceased as well. Her heart sped nervously, and she called out to the night. "Who is there?" Straining to hear an answer, she heard the whispering rustle of silk, nothing more. More loudly, she called out again, "Please, who is it? May I pass in peace?"

A figure melted from what had seemed only mist, moving slowly and silently forward. It was a woman. Isabella's shoulders loosened somewhat. As the woman approached, Isabella caught sight of her eyes, tormented, anguished eyes, lost. Catching her breath, she reached out, wanting somehow to help.

"Who are you, lady, and what is wrong?" She asked, stepping forward. "May I help? I…"

The eyes were horrible in their pain. She felt drawn to them by more than compassion, unable to pull her gaze from their depths. Far, far too late, she forced her eyes down, down to where trembling lips parted, lips of deepest, darkest red, framing teeth that gleamed and sparkled with captured moonlight.

She struggled against the control of the eyes, against her fear. Her lips formed words, screams, any sound to negate the horror. They left her only a whisper, caught in the night breeze and borne away. The teeth were long, curved and sharp, inhuman. They drew nearer now with shock.

The morning dew misted on the chill, pale skin of Isabella's motionless form. She lay, awaiting the morning sun, broken and lifeless. There were twin punctures in the softness of her throat, and a ghastly contortion of absolute fear masked the innocent beauty of her face. There was no blood, but the shadows had lifted.

Judas 10:20

20 As he spoke, a ruler came to him and knelt before him, saying "My daughter has died. 21 Come and lay your hand upon her, and she shall live." 22 Jesus rose and followed him as did his disciples.

23 As he walked, a woman who had bled for twelve years reached out to touch his cloak. 24 She said to herself, "If only I touch his cloak, then I shall be healed."

25 Turning, Jesus saw her and said, "Take heart, daughter, for your faith has healed you." 26 And the woman was whole from that moment on.

27 When Jesus entered the ruler's house and saw the musicians and the noisy crowd, he moved them aside. 28 Seeing that no color remained to the girl's cheeks, and seeing also the marks upon her throat, he said, "Go away, for the girl is not dead, but only sleeping." 29 They laughed at him. 30 After they had been put outside, Jesus closed the door behind himself, barring it from within.

After touching the girl's throat, which was still and without pulse, Jesus felt a tug at his heart. A shadow passed the window, and he raised his eyes, now wet with tears, to meet those that faced him. Weeping also, the temptress only watched to see if he would smite her, removing the hunger, ending the pain.

"Why?" He asked simply, brushing the soft strands of the girl's hair with tender fingers.

"You heard the curse, Lord," she responded, unable to hide the bitterness in her words. "Lucifer saw in my heart that I would die for you. He took steps to insure that I could not. Each night the hunger grows. I am too weak to fight it. I seek only to follow you."

Feeling the sincerity in her words, Jesus heaved a sigh of deepest resignation, feeling suddenly the great weight thrust upon his shoulders.

"She may walk again," he said, simply, and the girl's eyes fluttered and opened. She did not smile; her expression was one of need--of desperation.

"Her lifeblood is now a part of me," the temptress spoke, each word catching at her heart. "She will hunger as I. You know this is true, why do you raise her to such torment?"

"I am the way, the truth, and the light," he said, slowly turning to the door. "Even in her torment, she is forgiven.

For every such horror unleashed upon my father's children, I shall exact threefold payment on the day of reckoning."

"And I," she breathed, fearing the answer to come, "am I forgiven, then?"

Staring deeply within her eyes, Jesus communed with her heart. Since the days when she had walked freely upon the roads of Heaven, she had felt nothing like it. His purity surrounded her, probed her, and then was gone.

"I shall call you Mary," he spoke. "Go with open heart, for we shall meet again." He turned then, leaving the room with the girl at his side, returning to the disciples and those who waited. Mary, for she gladly accepted the name, departed the window and melted through the crowd, going again into the desert to be alone. Only Judas, who had seen her at the window and noted her odd, exceptional beauty, noted her passing, and he was too much in awe at the miracle of the dead girl walking to dwell upon it.

Judas 10:31

31 A woman was seen to pass the window frame and to speak. 32 Taking the girl by the hand, Jesus led her outside, and she lived, though no spark remained to her eyes--except that of hunger--and her pallor was that of death. 33 All stood in awe, and the news spread rapidly throughout the land. 34 Ignoring her father and those about her, the girl walked into the desert and was seen no more.

Judas 13:9

9 When Jesus heard of the beheading of John the Baptist, he withdrew to a solitary place by boat. 10 Hearing this, a great crowd gathered and awaited his arrival, traveling there on foot. 11 Seeing them, Jesus had compassion on them and healed their sick.

12 As darkness began to fall, the disciples came to him saying, "This is a remote place, and the hour is already late.

Send the crowds away so that they can go the villages and buy something to eat."

13 Jesus replied, "There is no need for them to go away. We will give them something to eat." 14 "We have only five loaves of bread and two fish," they replied.

15 "Bring them to me," he said. Jesus directed the people to sit in the grass, and breaking the loaves, raised his eyes to the heavens and gave thanks. 16 Then he gave them to his disciples, who gave them to the people. They all ate, and were satisfied, and the disciples collected twelve basketfuls of pieces that were left over. 17 Those that were fed numbered about five thousand men, besides women and children.18 Immediately after, Jesus made the disciples get into the boat and go on ahead of him to the other side, while he dismissed the crowd. 19 After the people had departed, one woman remained, Mary of Magdalene, and they spoke at length.

As the crowds dispersed, Mary moved slowly forward, watching first from afar for any sign that she was not wanted. She had remained as long in the desert as her will could stand. Again the hunger was upon her. She stood, wavering, and watched as the son of Man bid farewell to his people. Her heart calmed somewhat, being close to him, but the aching need did not diminish. Slowly, he turned, seeing her as if from far away, and he came to stand by her side, watching as the last of the crowds disappeared into the distance.

"They have beheaded John," he said slowly, ignoring the plea in her eyes, "Truly these are evil times. Your master has sown well."

"What is death," she asked, eyes wide, "to one who serves you? It is the victory in the greatest of battles. I wish death would come to me in such service…I hunger again." With a great sadness in his eyes, he put his hands upon her shoulders. "You suffer because of me, as did John, and I feel your pain. The time is not yet upon us when I can offer you peace. You must follow, remaining close to my side, for I say unto you, the Son of Man is not like other men. You may feed upon me, for I shall not die."

Feeling the depth of the emotion in his words, and seeing the tears as they began streaming from his eyes, Mary turned and fled. He did not know, could not know, what might befall him if he offered her salvation. As one of the fallen, she knew only too well the fire of his father's wrath. She ran through the desert and into the villages, running until she could no longer concentrate her will upon flight--until the hunger overwhelmed her. Creeping through the shadows, she tried to rest, but inside her mind, Lucifer laughed, saying, "Mary, time to feed. The hunger will return you to me. It is greater than you, or he can conceive. It is my hunger, and I will feast."

Jesus climbed the mountain, sore of heart. She drew him, even then, and the weight of John's loss was heavy on his human heart. Stones cut his fingers and feet as he climbed, and the wind chilled him, but he ignored it all. He ascended to the uppermost ledge that he could reach and knelt upon the cold, dusty stone.

"Forgive me, father," he prayed, "but I have no answer for this one, now named Mary, and she is sorely beset. Your enemy controls her, but her heart is pure. Give me the strength, lead my steps, for I love her, and I would not see her, or any other, suffer."

Thunder echoed from the hills, lightning flashed, and still he prayed. No space remained in his father's heart for those cast out, no redemption was theirs. Jesus knew, and yet he prayed, for his heart was pure, and he bore no grudge against any who would be saved, no matter their sin. No answers were forthcoming, and he was forced to rise, finally, descending the mountain with heavy heart.

On the horizon, far from shore, he saw the boat with his disciples, his children. He stepped onto the surface of the water, walking slowly after the retreating sails, as waves slapped his legs and stung his cuts with their chill caress. .

Judas 13:29

29 During the fourth watch of the night, Jesus came to the boat, walking upon the lake. 30 Seeing this, the disciples were terrified. "It is a ghost," they said, crying out in fear.

31 But Jesus said to them: "Take courage, it is I! Do not be afraid."

32 "Lord," cried Peter, "If it is you, tell me to come to you on the water."

33 "Come," he said.

34 Then Peter left the boat, walking on the water toward Jesus. 35 Seeing the wind and the splashing of the waves, he became frightened, and began to sink. 36 Crying out, he said, "Lord, save me!"

37 Jesus reached out his hand, pulling him from the waves, and said, "Oh you of little faith, why did you doubt?" 38 And when they climbed into the boat the wind died down. 39 Then those who were in the boat worshipped him saying, "Truly you are the son of God."

40 Then Judas, still confused over the woman, Mary, asked, "Lord, why do you consort with a woman plagued by demons? Shall you not cleanse the world of darkness?"

41 Jesus looked at him and spoke a parable: "If you take a candle and light it in the darkness, it can be seen for many miles. 42 Light the same candle in the sun's rays, and it pales to nothing. 43 I am sent to show the path to my father's lost sheep. She is among them. 44 I say to you, only in the last days shall evil and darkness be washed away, for in their very darkness, they glorify the light of the heavens."

45 So saying, he fell silent, and spoke to no man as long as they were upon the boat."

Judas 15:20

20 About eight days after saying this, Jesus took Peter, John, and James with him and went onto a mountain to pray. 21 As he prayed, the appearance of his face changed and his clothing became bright, like a flash of lightning. 22 Two men, Elijah and Moses, appeared in glorious splendor, talking with Jesus. 23 They spoke of his departure, which he was about to bring to fulfillment in Jerusalem. 24 They spoke as well of the temptress, Mary, whose soul Jesus would save. 25 There were looks of sadness on the faces of his companions, then, for they knew the father's heart was hardened to the fallen, and they feared now for his son. 26 They had no answer for him, though they bid him not to fear. 27 Peter and his companions were very sleepy, but when they became fully awake, they saw his glory, and the two men standing with him. 28 As the men were leaving Jesus, Peter said, "Lord, it is good for us to be here. Let us put up three shelters, one for you, one for Moses, and one for Elijah. (He knew not what he said)29 While he spoke, a cloud appeared, enveloping them all, and they were afraid. 30 A voice came from the cloud, saying, "This is my son, whom I have chosen. Heed his words." 32 When the voice had spoken, the cloud dispersed, and they were alone with Jesus, who had tears in his eyes.

33 The apostles decided to keep this to themselves, and told no one what they had seen, or heard, at that time.

Judas 17:1

1 A man named Lazarus was sick. He was from Bethany, the village of Mary and her sister Martha. This Mary, whose brother Lazarus now lay sick, was the same who had poured perfume on the Lord and washed his feet with her hair. 2 The sisters sent word to Jesus saying, "Lord, one you love is dying."

3 "This sickness shall not end in death," Jesus said, "No; it is for God's glory, so that God's son may be glorified by it." 4 Jesus loved Mary, Martha, and Lazarus, yet upon hearing the nature of the illness; he waited two days before going to them. 5 There were reports that Lazarus bore strange punctures on his throat, and his pallor was deathly and pale.6 Then he said to his disciples, "Let us go back to Judea."

7 But Rabbi," they said, "a short while ago the Jews tried to stone you, and yet you are going back there?"

8 "There are twelve hours of daylight," Jesus answered, "a man who walks by daylight will not stumble, for he sees by this world's light. It is when he walks by night that he stumbles, for he has no light."

9 After saying this, he went on to explain. "Our friend Lazarus has fallen asleep, I go to awaken him."

10 His disciples replied, "Lord, if he sleeps, he will get better." 11 Jesus spoke of death, but they did not understand.

12 Then he said plainly, "Lazarus is dead, and for your sake, I am glad I was not there, so that your faith may grow. 13 Let us go to him, for the darkness from which he must awaken is of my own creation, and there is another there whom I seek.

14 Then Thomas said, "Come, let us follow that we may die with him."

When the word of Jesus' return reached the sisters, Martha hurried out to meet him. Mary, deep in mourning, would not leave the house. She babbled of dark, shadowed women, and blood, and many feared she was either mad, or possessed of demons.

"Lord," Martha pleaded, as she arrived at his side, "If you had been here, I know my brother would not have died. Even now, I know, whatever you ask, God shall give it to you." Jesus saddened, doubting this in his heart, but he answered, "Your brother shall rise again."

Martha answered, "I know he will rise in the last days, at the resurrection."

Jesus said to her, "I am the resurrection and the life. He who believes in me will live, even though he dies. Whoever lives and believes in me will never die. Do you believe this?"

"Yes, Lord," she replied, falling to her knees and brushing his legs with her hair, eyes wide. "I believe you are The Christ, son of God, who has come to the earth as a man."

"Where is your sister, Mary?" He asked.

"I will send her to you, Lord," Martha answered, rising. "She is mad with grief, speaking of demons and shadows and afraid to walk, even in daylight."

"I shall comfort her," he said, seating himself on a stone to wait. "Send her to me."

Martha rushed back to her sister's side with Jesus' message, hope blooming in her heart. She had lost her brother already. She did not wish to lose Mary as well.

When Mary heard that Jesus had come, she rose, as though frightened, and ran from the house, much to Martha's shock. Several of the others there, believing Mary was going to Lazarus's tomb to mourn, followed a short distance behind.

Mary's breath came in short gasps, and the sharp stones of the road cut into her feet as she ran. Every three or four paces she looked over her shoulder, eyes wide with fear, searching the pockets of shadow surrounding the trail. Her heart pounded wildly in her breast, threatening to burst from her skin. Stumbling into the grouped disciples, she staggered to Jesus, falling to the ground at his feet, sobbing.

Reaching down, Jesus took her by the hands and raised her to face him. "What is wrong, Mary?" He asked, searching her tear-stained face. Her entire body trembled, like that of a frightened colt, ready to bolt and run.

"Lord," she choked out, dragging huge gulps of air into her lungs, "Lord, my brother has been killed by a demon!"

Jesus showed no doubt, only asked what she meant, and she answered, "She came in the night. I saw her twice, a woman wearing only a cloak of shadows. She drank of his blood, Lord, leaving him weaker with each visit. She had fangs. Lord, I am frightened for my brother's soul!"

"Take me to where you have laid him," Jesus said, "and fear not."

When they reached the place, a cave which had been sealed by the placement of a very large stone, Jesus looked upon it and wept. The people who had followed Mary in her flight saw this and said, "See how Jesus loved him?"

But Jesus cried only a little for Lazarus. His heart was heavy with the knowledge of who was responsible, with the weight of another soul. The face of the temptress, Mary, haunted his thoughts, her fate haunted his tears. He turned to Mary, Lazarus's sister.

"Have them remove the stone, daughter," he said.

"But Lord," she protested, eyes wide, "it has been four days! Already the smell of rot will be upon him...why must we do this?"

And Jesus, weary of heart, replied, "Did I not tell you that, if you believed, you would witness my father's glory? Open the tomb."

Judas 18:39

39 So they took away the stone. Then Jesus looked up and said, "Father, in all things you hear me. I say this not for myself, but for those standing here, that they may believe you have sent me."

40 When he had said this, Jesus called out in a loud voice, "Lazarus, come forth." 41 The dead man came out, his hands and feet wrapped in strips of linen, and a cloth binding his face.

42 Jesus said, "Take off the grave clothes, and let him go."

And Lazarus, staggering in the sunlight, came forth from his tomb. The wind billowed his stringy hair about his head, and his eyes glowed with the light of hunger. Facing Jesus, he removed the shroud from his face, revealing the white, pale skin beneath. When he smiled, all present shuddered and backed away. His teeth, glistening in the light, were pointed, like those of a serpent. "Son of man," he called, "you have granted me that I may walk again, though the price is great. Why must I suffer so?"

And Jesus, speaking slowly and clearly, answered. "When the last days come, your soul shall be remembered. Know that I am with you, go in peace." "I will go, but in hunger, not peace," the dead man snarled, glaring about at those assembled in hatred. Then there was a flash of mist, pungent with the cloying scent of open graves and death, and when it cleared, Lazarus was gone. Only the empty tomb remained.

Jesus, weeping openly again, pulled the sisters, Martha and Mary, to his side and comforted them, wiping the fear from their hearts with his touch. Gesturing to his disciples, he bid them stay with the crowd, and he went off after Lazarus.

He found the dead man in the shadows of an old well. "Lazarus," he called out, "come to me!" Unable to resist, the dead man complied. "What now, Son of Man," he called out in fear. "Have you come to kill the evil you have created, now that they have seen? Was it only a show for their benefit, the casting aside of my soul?"

The words cut deeply, and Jesus' voice trembled as he answered. He knew that what he was about to do was not a part of his father's plan. He could not help his heart, though, and was unable to witness Lazarus's suffering.

"Come to me, Lazarus," he said, tilting his head to one side, "for I have promised that you will live, and I know of your hunger and she who brought it upon you. Feed you from the blood of the Son of Man, and be renewed. Fear not, I shall not die, for it is not yet my time."

Lazarus gazed in wonder, backing away at first, but the temptation to sate his need was too great, and the power of Jesus' voice compelled him. Drawing near, he leapt wildly, sinking his fangs deeply into flesh and causing Jesus to stagger, moaning from the pain. Despite the agony, Jesus stood quietly, and moments later, Lazarus stopped, stumbling backward to collapse on the sand.

Recovering quickly, and causing his own wounds to heal, Jesus gathered Lazarus into his arms and returned the way he had come. The man he carried, no longer pale, breathed easily. Lazarus lived, though the spark in Jesus' eyes was a bit dimmer, and his steps slightly uneven. Delivering Lazarus to his sisters, he said, "Take him home, for he must rest. I have cast forth his demon, and he is whole. Now I, too, must rest."

Seeing that Lazarus' teeth were those of a normal man, and that he slept peacefully, the crowd murmured in wonder, and rushed to spread the news of what he had done.

As the crowds left them, Jesus called aside his disciple, Judas Iscariot, and spoke to him alone.

"Go to the village," he said, "find the woman, Mary of Magdalene, and bring her to me."

"But Lord," Judas said, frightened for his master, "she has followed us, and where she goes, evil goes as well. Why must I bring her here?"

"She loves me, as do you, Judas," Jesus replied. "Her evil is my burden. Go quickly, for I must see her in the darkness. Do not tell the others, for I would not put my own weight upon their hearts."

Casting aside his fear as best as possible, Judas went into the village. The other disciples, knowing that Judas carried the purse, assumed that he went to purchase food, and asked no questions. Darkness was falling swiftly, chilling the air and silencing the sounds of life. Judas' heart hammered wildly, and his footsteps quickened. It was nearly the ninth hour when he came across Mary, seated in a garden and watching the night — as though expecting him.

"Hello, Judas," she called out, beckoning him closer.

"Why are you abroad, alone, on such a night? Has your master no use for you?"

"He has sent me for you, Lady, though I know not why," Judas replied. Her presence drew him like a magnet, calling out to his senses. His skin heated, and he blushed.

"Do you fear me, Judas?" She asked, no smile in her eyes.

"Lady, I do," he replied, avoiding her eyes. "Will you come? He is waiting."

"If he calls, I will come," she answered, rising with a rustle of linen that melted Judas' loins. "But I tell you, Judas, for my sake he risks everything, and I am saddened, for I, too, love him."

"I pray thee, Mary," Judas burst out, spinning to brave the depths of her eyes, "do not come. Stay away from him. I fear for him, and I fear you."

She smiled then, but he felt no trace of sincere emotion from her heart. He froze in shock at the hunger of her gaze, the misery so obvious in the expression of her face. It was bitter, overwhelming, threatening to swallow him. Then she averted her eyes, and she began walking. He could only follow.

When they were near to where Jesus lay, he bid her wait, and, entering the camp, he came to his master and spoke. "She has come, Lord; I have left her just beyond the camp."

"It is good," Jesus replied, rising. "Tell any who asks that I am in the desert, praying. Do not fear for me, Judas, for I have said, it is not yet my time. Fear instead for Mary, for I am not certain of her fate."

And Jesus walked into the shadows, leaving Judas alone to kneel and pray.

She waited for him in shadows, watching him approach with hooded eyes. His steps were firm and steady, and a glow encased his features. She trembled as she felt the brush of his nearness, cowering deeper into the blackness.

"Mary," he commanded, stopping and staring unerringly into the darkness, "come forth, for the time is upon us that I must begin to bear your burden."

She wanted to break free, to run, but she was his to command, and she could not. He stood, arms wide, waiting, and he beckoned her forth. She came, haltingly at first, then rushing--blowing across the sand like a dark wind, and they embraced.

"I will take from you your hunger," he whispered, cupping her face in his hands and staring into her eyes in love, "and you shall have a part of what is mine, that you may be saved."

"You cannot know what he will do! Your father will not be pleased!" She pleaded with him, even as he directed her, placing her lips to his throat and caressing her teeth with his skin.

"My father's will be done," he said, eyes brimming with trapped emotion, "I will not allow any to suffer. Drink, Mary, for the hour is late, and my days here are now few."

And the hunger swept aside her objections as he spoke. She plunged her fangs deep, drank richly of his lifeblood, weeping as she fed, and he moaned from the pain, yet caressed her hair softly, eyes closed in prayer.

Watching from nearby, Judas shrank away in horror. Rushing to the camp, he looked about wildly for his weapons, waking the others in his frantic haste.

"What is it?" Peter asked, grabbing his arm. "Where is our Lord?"

"He is in the desert!" Judas cried, "beset by a demon! We must go to him!"

And they all rushed out then, some only partially clothed, bearing swords and spears. Judas led them quickly through the shadows to where he had seen Jesus and Mary. When they arrived, however, they found only their Lord, seated, head bowed in prayer.

"Master," Peter cried, "Judas said that you were beset by a demon, so we have come to you!" Looking up, eyes very tired and voice weak, Jesus answered. "There is no demon here, but I am weary. Lead me to the camp, for I must rest."

Eyes full of wonder, for they had never seen their Lord in such a state, they raised him between them and carried him to his bed, where he fell asleep immediately. In the shadows behind them, weeping, yet marveling at her near-human skin and the peace in her heart, Mary watched them go. Turning, she ran back to the village. The night swallowed her quickly, and the desert was once more still.

Judas 21:1

1 When he had finished praying, Jesus left with his disciples and crossed the Kidron valley. 2 On the other side was an olive grove, and Jesus and his disciples entered it.

3 Judas, sent to the village for food, met with the woman, Mary of Magdalene, and was delayed in coming to the grove. 4 As he neared the place, he saw Peter in conference with several armed men. 5 The soldiers, accompanied by officials from the Priests and Pharisees, entered the grove just after Judas, who bore a message from Mary. 6 Kissing his master on the cheek, he whispered the words he had been given. 7 Then the soldiers stepped forward and the disciples grew silent.8 "Who is it you seek?" Jesus asked, knowing all that would come to pass.

9 "Jesus of Nazareth," they replied.

10 "I am he," Jesus said.

11 Peter, attempting to hide his betrayal, drew his sword and struck the High Priest's servant, severing his ear. (The servant's name was Malchus) 12 Jesus said, "Put that sword away. Shall I deny the cup my father pours me?"

13 Turning to the Pharisees and soldiers, Jesus said, "Am I leading a rebellion, then, that you need come upon me by stealth, with swords and clubs? 14 I sat teaching in your courtyards every day, yet you did not arrest me. 15 This has come about that the prophecies may be fulfilled."
16 Then all his disciples deserted him and fled.

In great anger, Judas followed Peter in his flight. When they reached a point far enough away from the soldiers for safety, he grabbed his fellow disciple's shoulder, spinning him roughly.

"What have you done, Peter?" He demanded. Peter's eyes were haunted, distant, and Judas recoiled from them in horror.

"He looked well in chains, do you not think so?" The voice was cold, like brittle ice, cracking through the air. It was not Peter's voice, nor was it any human expression that rode the familiar features.

"Who are you?" Judas asked, backing away, "You are not Peter!"

"I am more than your mind can grasp, fool," the demon voice chuckled, "more than even your master imagines. Perhaps he is coming to some knowledge of this, even now!"

Lowering his gaze to avoid the eyes, which glittered with unnatural light and gripped at his heart, Judas began to pray. The demon, jeering and dark, ranted at him, giving no reprise. Steeling himself, Judas ignored the voice, falling to his knees in the sand.

"Our father, who art in heaven," he began, "be with your servant in his hour of need. Free my brother from this evil, return to us Simon, called Peter, for our Lord needs us now, your son, unworthy as we are, and I have not the strength alone."

As his courage grew, he rose, raising his eyes to those of his tormentor, searching for his brother.

"You are too weak." the demon's voice seemed to waver. "I leave of my own will, not that of your accursed father, or his six-mothered bastard. And I leave you a gift. Your brethren will believe you the cause of your master's death. Your kiss will become the symbol of his betrayal!"

"Get thee hence!" Judas staggered forward, as if his physical presence alone could intimidate the evil confronting him. Peter's features contorted, rippled between despairing, imploring humanity, and gripping, snarling darkness. As Judas's fingers touched Peter's shoulders, there was a sound like the rushing of a great wind, and they were both struck to the ground. When the demon had passed, leaving swirling pillars of sand in its wake, they rose slowly, blinking their eyes and checking their bones.

"We must follow our Lord, for they have taken him," Judas said, turning away. Peter watched him, a glare in his eye. His expression, accusing and dark, was more painful than even the demon's gaze had been, for it shone through the disciple's own features, and rose from his own mind. Judas trembled, remembering the words, "Your kiss will become the symbol of his betrayal."

Peter followed, but did not speak. The ominous weight of his silence bore down upon Judas like a smothering fog, but still he walked on. It was a small price, he told himself, for his brother's soul... Tears burned with the swirling sand down his cheeks, and dried instantly, wisping into the eye of the sun.

Judas 25:17

17 The soldiers took Jesus into their charge. Carrying upon his shoulder his own cross, he went out to Golgotha (called the place of the skull) 18 Here they crucified him, along with two others--one to each side, with Jesus in the middle. 19 Pilate had a notice prepared and fastened to the cross. It read:

JESUS OF NAZARETH, THE KING OF THE JEWS.

20 It was lettered in Aramaic, Latin, and Greek, and many Jews read the sign, for the place of the crucifixion was near the city. 21 The Chief Priests of the Jews protested, saying, "Do not write, 'The King of the Jews,' but instead that this man claimed to be the King of the Jews."

22 Pilate answered, "I have written what I have written."23 When the soldiers had crucified Jesus, they took his clothes, dividing them into four equal shares, one for each of them, with the undergarment remaining. 24 This remaining garment was without seams, woven in one piece. 25 "Let's not tear it," they said to one another. "Let's decide by lot who will get it."

26 This happened that the Scripture might be fulfilled which said,
'They divided my garments among them
And cast lots for my clothing.'
29 So this is what the soldiers did.

30 Near the cross of Jesus stood his mother, his mother's sister, Mary, wife of Clopas, and Mary Magdalene. 31 When Jesus saw his mother there, and the disciple whom he loved, (Peter), and she for whom he wept, he said to his mother, "Dear woman, here is your son," and to the disciple, "Here is your mother." 32 To Mary Magdalene he said, "You are one with my heart. Though my father calls, I will be with you. Do not forget." 33 From that time on, the disciple took Jesus' mother into his home. 34 Mary Magdalene, hearing the Lord's words, wept bitterly, unable to stand his pain.

Darkness fell upon the threefold wooden frames, trailing shadowy tendrils among the rivulets of blood that clotted and grew sticky on his skin. Jesus regarded those below in the weaving, half-coalesced vision of his pain. Tears dried, unwilling to remoisten his cheeks. He remained conscious only through continuous, jumbled prayer, chasing the tumbling words and thoughts through his heart and pressing them outward to his father with all the strength of his will. None answered. It was done. He'd dared to presume himself above his father's disfavor, reached out to one beyond his power, and he'd given of the greatest gift he'd received to one beyond redemption--desecrating himself in the eyes of his own father.

He could feel his strength ebbing. The pain was beyond anything he'd experienced before, beyond even the pain of his father's disapproval. The human body he wore neared death, and it spoke of this eloquently. So hard, he thought, such a weight to bear. How do they retain faith? And what have I done, taking my gift of salvation and flinging it aside as if it were mine alone?

"I...I am thirsty," he croaked at last, beseeching those below.

A plant stem was raised, topped by a sponge, and he greedily sucked on the moistness, feeling the bitter sting as the wine-vinegar trickled down his parched throat.

Pulling his face from the sponge weakly, he raised his eyes to the sky and cried out, hurling the words from deep inside his breast, calling out loudly.

"My father, why have you forsaken me?"

And life slipped from his body at that moment, leaving him limp and unmoving on the skeletal framework of the cross.

Mary, seeing that it was truly death that was upon him, screamed a terrible scream, an impotent, nerve-grinding wail to a God she could not reach. Those around her fled from her fury, crying out in fear and racing for homes and fires. She paid them no heed.

He had risked it all, all that he was, for her, for her soul, and the risk had been in vain--he was dead! He had walked the Earth as the Son of God, but, having given to her of his gift, having fed her a part of himself, he had died as a man, and all he had lived was wiped away as if it had never been. In that instant, prophecy was cast to the winds without thought. Still screaming, she ran to the desert, pulling at her almost human hair and cursing the sky with raging torrents of unchecked emotion. Deep within her, sparked by her loss of control, a dark voice reached out to her, laughing the mocking laughter of the victor.

Unable to go on, she dropped to her knees, and, fighting back the encroaching darkness in her soul, she began--for the first time since her feet touched the earth—to pray, loudly and blindly. He had given himself for her, for her salvation, though it cost the world. She prayed for only the chance to return his love, to replace his gift. She continued to pray, unaware of her surroundings, while a glowing figure appeared at her side. She did not notice that she was not alone until his fingers brushed her shoulder.

Stifling a cry, she backed away, half-rising to her feet. Elijah stood before her, resplendent, but with sorrow beyond comprehension on his features--sadness beyond measure.

"Woman, now called Mary," he spoke, "would you truly return the light?"

"I..." she lowered her eyes, bowing in supplication, "I would release to you my soul to return him--to fulfill his prophecy. I would do anything."

"Go you then" the voice instructed, "and find Judas, who they name betrayer. Tell him all. In his lifeblood, and in his love, you will find the strength. If you willingly replace the gift of the Son of Man with Judas' mortal blood, your curse will return. In that hour shall all be righted...go and may we all be judged on a standard such as your love."

The light was gone, the darkness remained, and Mary rose, returning through the sifting shadows to the cross. Tears streamed steadily down her cheeks, dampening the locks of her hair, and her steps were uneven. It was too great a cost. She had been granted that which no other could give a second time, and now it was demanded of her to return it...she clutched her arms tightly to her stomach to ease the churning and the pain. In her mind, echoing voices mocked her feeble will, laughed at her lack of courage. Already Lucifer and his minions counted the victory won. She was lost to them, but The Christ was lost to mankind. Wailing her despair, she ran on, finding Judas just before the dawning sun rose to the horizon. He knelt alone, lost in prayer of his own. He did not see her coming, and she watched him for a long moment before speaking.

Judas 28:1

1 And Judas Iscariot, blamed of the betrayal, prayed in the darkness. 2 The temptress, she called Mary Magdalene, came upon him, wild of eye, and cheeks damp with tears, crying out, "Judas, beloved or our Lord, a great evil has come upon us."

3 "Lady," Judas replied, "in three days our Lord shall rise from his grave, redemption is at hand."

4 "He is dead," she told him, seating herself, "of love for me, he sacrificed all. We bear the weight, you and I, for I have spoken with Elijah, and he has sent me to you."

5 And she spoke to him of Lucifer, and of her curse, and of Jesus' gift of life, with its terrible price. 6 They wept, clinging to one another, and Judas cried out, "The weight is too great on you, Mary, for he would not wish you to pay this price!"

7 "That," she replied, "is why I must pay it."

8 "Then take me," Judas lay back, baring his throat, tears in his own eyes, "for truly your love rivals even his, and his gift is too precious to lose."

9 Seeing the love in Judas's eyes, feeling the wrench of Satan's very claws as he leapt to prevent her, the woman, Mary, fell upon the body of Judas and fed, the curse taking her even as she swept forward. Weeping, she cast herself willingly to the darkness from which she'd been raised, feeling the icy claws of the hunger that would once again consume her.

10 Sated, she rose, and Judas also, now pale and alight with hunger of his own, and they fled as Lucifer hunted them, possessed of a great and futile rage. 11 As darkness engulfed them, they shared one last glance--a last time they smiled. 12 Then it was black, and they were smitten with the fire of Lucifer, losing all thought.

When Mary and Judas regained consciousness, they both awoke to hunger. Fighting it back, screaming inwardly with the fire of their need, they walked, side by side, through twilight three days beyond Jesus' death. Silence filled the night. All those who lived nearby either slept, or were sitting home. They reached the place where Jesus' tomb lay without meeting a soul, coming to stand by the huge stone that had blocked his return to the world. A fear gnawed at the depth their breasts, nearly smothered, but burning still.

Standing within, gazing at them through haloed prisms, formed of the brilliance of his glory, seen through the mirrors of his tears, the Son of Man regarded them with great sadness, and endless love.

Their own eyes, devoid of natural light, flickered with the pain of loss, and the wonder of the intensity of his love. No word did they speak, only awaited their fate and drank in the sight of their Lord.

"Though I suffer not your curse, I will be with you," Jesus spoke. "A time will come when I walk these roads again--you will be there, and I will remember."

Turning, Mary Magdalene and Judas Iscariot, called traitor, fled into the darkness, overcome with hunger and pain, tethered in the cutting bonds of evil. Alone once more, Jesus stood, weeping tears of glittering sadness to wet the sand at his feet. They blurred his sight. Time was so short. He could not follow them, could do nothing but accept their sacrifice. It should have been his alone. He turned, walking forth to embrace the world.

Judas: 30

1 Running from the tomb, where Jesus stood, resurrected, Judas stole a length of rope from a nearby home. 2 Coming upon a tall tree, he cast it upon a sturdy branch. 3 Putting to the end of the rope a noose, he climbed to a branch high above the ground, fixed the rope to his neck, and leapt, hanging himself.4 Finding him thus, the people spoke against him, led by Simon, called Peter, saying, "He has taken his life from shame, for he betrayed his Lord."5 Mary Magdalene, running to where the disciples were gathered, said, "I have seen the Lord, and he is risen."

6 And Jesus appeared other times to his disciples, speaking words of comfort and salvation, and was raised once more to his throne in Heaven. 7 We, who hunger, remain. 8 The rope has failed to relieve me of my burden. 9 In the bark of the tree where we left the rope, Mary inscribed the words, "Here hung one who loves beyond life."10

May God forgive us."

Miracles in the Night

I have traveled roads long and weary, darkness my companion and destiny my guide. I have seen the sun rise and set on the courts of kings, and I have seen those kingdoms crumble back to dust. I have shared wine with women, war with men, and the night with no one. I have no name, and yet I am. Death does not stalk me; not though I dream a thousand nights for his cold embrace. This is my destiny.

Though I was born to poverty and ignorance, I have aspired to eloquence and power. I am a success story on an epic scale, one with a tragic footnote. This story I have put down that those who follow in my footsteps will understand that I was here, that I endure, even now, even in the social wasteland of this place that they now call Norfolk, but that has none of the charm, or the old-world civility, of the original city of that name.

I came here out of boredom, out of an incessant need for travel, a yearning for change. I have spoken with derelicts, madmen so soused on wine and midnight dreams that they could barely remember their given names, but whose words wove the tapestry of society with clarity and vision. I have stalked men and women as well, from upper to lower class, knowing each, loving few, ending the existences of all but one. That is my story.

I prowled the docks, for they are near the sea, near those whose adventuresome souls and yearning hearts mirror in some small way the eternal quest that drives me onward. The men of these later days do not have the heart, or the strength, of those whom I knew in earlier times—in greater times—but the spirit is still there, and it was that I sought. Something different, something new. Someone who might relieve the unbearable weight of boredom that bears down on my shoulders every waking moment of the night. I never dreamed of entertainment, I sought only a moment's relief.

I thought momentarily of the bars. There is always music. Caustic and violent as the modern groups tended to be, there was still the allure of poetry, still the message of their souls to be picked free. I decided against it. It was a night to wander beneath the stars, to find something unique. Somehow I felt it, and I have learned to trust my instincts.

And so the docks—the waves—the moonlight dancing on choppy, off-shore swells and glistening in the captured pools of salt-spray on the rocks. I moved as silently as the breeze, as effortlessly as the gulls who owned the day-time sky.

I dream, at times, of those moments—the price of immortality—the daylight lives and trivial pursuits of those upon whom I fed. I can remember, even now, the graceful swooping movements of birds, their arrogant cries. Such dreams are an empty pursuit—painful.

I saw him as I crossed from one darkened alley to another, walking along a row of abandoned warehouses without concern, despite the hour and the solitude—despite the danger. We were not in one of the better neighborhoods, those held no interest to me. It was the edge of things, the borders of the "real" world, that caught at my senses and gave me a reason to go on.

From the instant he caught my eye, I knew I'd found what I was looking for. He wore what appeared to be a robe, sweeping to the ground at his feet. It was sewn and patched together of a hundred colored rags, of old shirts and pants, even socks, washcloths, towels and sheets. It was multicolored and ragged, and in the moonlight, with his long gray hair and unruly beard, with the staff he held in his right hand as he moved, he might have been an ancient prophet, Moses with his robe of many colors moving through the night.

I swept past him far to one side, coming at him from the front, where he could see me clearly, moving slowly and watching him with wondering eyes.

He never flinched. His eyes were filled with light and energy, the one thing about him that bore witness to an intelligence buried beneath the veneer of madness, of secrets he knew and none would guess. I smiled, and as I drew near, I held out my hand.

He stared at me, not offering his own hand in return, but he stopped as well, as though he'd spotted, or guessed at, my own nature. He did not turn to run, nor did he cower, but he stood there as an equal, calm and self-assured.

"You are Death?" he asked calmly?

I shook my head. "I am not, nor are you Moses, but there is a strange light about you."

"I am a prophet," he said matter-of-factly. "I have seen things—many things. They will not listen."

"They never have," I told him. "From one who knows only too well, they never have. Walk with me?" I asked him, but there was not really a question involved. He moved at my side easily, comfortably.

"I did not think you were Death," he told me, "because I have not yet foreseen my own."

"You see everything?" I prompted.

"No, only that which matters. To me, life matters very much, so I believe I will see Death, and I will know him."

"You are not so far from the mark," I admitted slowly. "I have been as the angel of death to many—too many to count. Does that frighten you?"

"No," he answered immediately. "Death is for all—I have always known that. If you were Death, I would walk with you anyway—what would be the point in resistance?"

"You are a religious man?" I asked, thoroughly intrigued. We were moving back toward the beach, along the water now. There were the flashing lights of boats—naval vessels—and the occasional backfire of a car's engine as backdrop to our conversation—nothing more.

"I am a religious man," he replied, his eyes growing far away, "In a sacrilegious land. I am a prophet in a world of non-believers. I am the answer to questions better left unanswered, and so, am unwanted as well. There is no soul in mankind any longer."

"And yet you believe in your own?"

"I live within my soul. It is my soul that draws me onward, that shows me ways when others see walls, that opens windows where others see only air. There are veils, shuttered portals all around us, but we have trained ourselves to ignore them. There are windows to the soul, but man has bricked them over.

"There is poetry, still, but it is empty. It is re-played pain and endless unfulfilled dreams. They do not know what will fulfill them, so they build towers to reach a God they do not believe in, hoping that when they arrive they can take over and all will be well.

"There is religion in the world, but there is no passion. The passion is for things of the Earth, things of the flesh. There is no passion for spirit, or for beauty. There is more passion for death—it must be pleasant for you?"

He turned to me then, and I was fascinated. "There is no passion in death, so it is not such a pleasant thing. I take no pleasure in death, my own or those of others. Death is a necessity, to me, the universe, even to you.

"I serve no Gods but the night, the stars, and hunger—only one demands anything of me and the effort necessary to please him is slight. Your Gods, it would seem, deny you nothing except life."

"I have more life here," he gestured to his breast, his eyes softening for a moment, almost twinkling, "than you will find in the rest of this city. I learn, I watch, I survive. These are my life. To know is enough."

"But it would be better if they knew, as well," I countered. "That is why you try to make them see."

"I tell them because they ask. Then they laugh, point their fingers, and wander back into darkness. It is not for me to judge, or to desire, but for them."

The hunger was calling to me, and I knew that if I stayed longer, much as I was enjoying this exchange, that I would feed. Something within me would not allow it. There was something in his eyes, something that reminded even me, after centuries of cynicism and loneliness, of faith. There was a promise in those eyes, and I would not snatch it from the Earth.

"I must leave you now," I told him. "To you I am not Death this night, but there are others. Walk your paths, prophesy and speak when they will listen.

"Our roads are not so different. We are solitary, we are visionary, and we are free. They are lonely roads, but they are true—keep that nearest to your heart."

With those words, and looking back only once into the flashing depths of his eyes, and then I was gone. I moved as swiftly as my heightened strength and agility would allow, beyond the limits of his sight—or perhaps not. He raised his staff, and he waved in the direction in which I'd moved. I did not return that wave, but turned to embrace the darkness with new vigor.

Somewhere behind me, a beacon, a latter-day Moses, walked the streets of his own land, showing miracles to the blind and preaching to the deaf. I moved as he named me, the Angel of Death, the Grim Reaper with fangs as my scythe and hunger as my guide. We both blended with the darkness.

All around me the blood called to me. Somewhere in the shadows of the city the renewal of my own form of life pulsed through another's veins. For once, I would dine with a clear conscience—I had spared a life that mattered, and he had shared that life with me of his own free will. Such are the miracles of the night.

On the Third Day

There is a slight mechanical whir as the projector snaps to life. Millions of tiny dust motes, seemingly transfixed by the brilliant beam, float past the lens as the leader continues to unwind. Three pairs of eyes focus on the screen. The emotions reflected in each are different, but no less intense.

Sea-green eyes radiate deep-seated apprehension, curiosity tinged with skepticism. Dark brown hair rings a taut, serious countenance. Small furrows map years of compassion, years of patient faith, and frequent smiles. Father Prescott's heartbeat is speeded. His mind is awhirl with conflicting doubt and wonder. Hands grasping his knees firmly, he leans forward intently.

Slate grey, predatory, the second set of eyes watches with a gleam of triumph, waiting—poorly shielded—for affirmation. Affirmation of control. Affirmation of a reality made comfortable by decades of normality. Cardinal Michaels knows anticipation of a different kind... anticipation of relief. His fingers are steepled and his posture relaxed. His countenance is austere. His snow-white hair waves over the collar of immaculate robes. Only the slightest hint of tension mars the utter assurance of his expression. It is not yet strong enough to be labeled doubt, but it is there.

Dark brown, open wide, the third set of eyes is awash with pain. They are surrounded by the footprints of stress—of self-recrimination—deep, wrinkled trails. They sag from lack of sleep, but are bright with the light of hope. Father Thomas does not anticipate the film—he has lived it. His eyes are not focused on the screen. Not yet. They dart to either side nervously, seeking the others—seeking answers. He meets no returning glance, and, like nails to a magnet, his eyes flick back to his memories as they dance before him across the screen. The others watch. Across time, Father Thomas returns to his nightmare—his blessing—his pain. He returns for judgment.

It was Good Friday, two days from Easter Sunday. It would be Father Thomas' third Easter mass since his arrival at the tiny chapel that had once been the cathedral of San Marcos on the coast of San Valencez, California. The bishop had long since moved to more fitting surroundings, leaving the small church to its parish of fruit farmers and tourists. It was his first parish. He was five minutes into the sacrament when he felt the itch. Sweat began to slowly coat his brow. He scanned the ocean of upturned faces—passed over them to the rear of the building. A flash of scarlet, a short stand, looking out of place, barely clearing the edge of a private balcony caught his gaze... held it for a moment... slipped away as the itch began to burn toward pain.

It was happening again, just as it had the previous year. But it was beginning sooner. The pain seemed somehow more intense, yet he knew that it was the same. The difference sat, cold and unforgiving, fifty feet above the back pew. Cardinal Michaels, grey eyes flashing even over such a great distance, watched and waited. The camera, seated on its tripod beside the Cardinal, caught candlelight and glittered like a third eye—also watching. Emotionless.

As before, it began with his wrists. First there were small red circles, about half the diameter of a dime. Father Thomas did not look at them. Instead, he clenched his hands so tightly to the sides of his pulpit that all blood was instantly drained. Bones popped. He continued to recite the mass. He could feel the red patches brushing the insides of his robes—growing redder—growing deeper—unaffected by the exertion of his will. He groaned as they began to eat through tendons, to rupture veins, barely managing to twist the sounds that involuntarily escaped his throat back to the words of the sacrament in time to mask the pain from his congregation. Small rivulets of bright red blood began to trickle down from his wrists. He could feel them as they ran beneath the silken sleeves of his robes.

Beads of moisture were forming on his brow, as well—thick, sticky beads. It felt as though a stinging band was compressing his temples, shooting tiny pin-pricks of pain down nerve endings to blend subtly with the growing agony in his wrists. Salt stung his eyes, shifting the room before him to a blurred panorama of haloed, prismatic chaos. Still he continued. Somehow the words just went on, rolling from his lips, strong and resonant, crashing from the walls and the domed ceiling. He knew that it was no longer his voice alone. He wept. Somehow his quivering knees managed to support him.

Throughout the cathedral other voices rose in cries of fear and wonder. Men and women crossed themselves, falling to their knees on the soft carpet. Father Thomas could feel the weight of their eyes, locked to the anguish etched across his features. A rough, uneven band of red circled his head, seeping slowly downward, matting his hair and winding its way in sticky trails through the strands of his beard. It ran across his eyes, obscuring even the fuzzy sight that had remained to him. The sleeves of his robe had plastered themselves to his wrists and arms.

The pain rose and fell with each breath, jarred him with each new inflection of his voice. It grasped at his words with burning fingers, threatening to choke off the sound — to replace it with an eloquence of agony. He fought it. His arms were on fire. Impossible pressures assaulted him from invisible sources. His head shook, rocked by white-hot lances of pain. His body seemed heavy, dragging at his concentration. Twisting his tortured face heavenward, he sought the only solace he knew, reached out for the only strength that could sustain him. He was blind to the room before him. He was deaf to all but his own voice, and the thundering pounding of his own pulse. The words he had fought for scant moments before became his support.

He raised his arms in supplication, blood running freely down from the twin wounds in his wrists. He incanted the final verses, invoked the blessing, his voice raised to the force of a thunderclap. The sound, in contrast to the silence that followed, echoed through his mind, strobed by his racing heart. As he continued to stare blindly heavenward, a sudden flash of searing light drove him to his knees, cutting through blood, bone, and tissue to cleanse his sight. He saw those before him for one final second. He saw his own wonder mirrored in their eyes, blended with their fear. Then all was blessedly blank.

There were screams as his knees crumpled and he slumped to the floor, but Father Thomas did not hear them. With blood clotting and drying in his hair and crusting on his vestments, he lay before the altar, unconscious and breathing rapidly.

ON THE THIRD DAY

The old Cathedral of San Marcos was a beautiful building with walls of gleaming white stone that seemed to catch at the rays of early morning sunlight and cast them back to the ocean below. The sight of the waves, crashing endlessly on the rocky coast, never failed to move Father Thomas, not even after nearly four years of sunrises. It was a rare view of something constructed by man and bathed in the light of God's own creation—the sun. A moment of communion between earth and the heavens. Thomas had read that ancient priests had once believed one could absorb energy from the sunrise. Standing as he was on the balcony of the cathedral, he could almost believe it.

Easter was approaching rapidly—his fourth at San Marcos. He could remember the last, a year past, as if it were yesterday. He had awakened in his room in the rear of the cathedral to weakness and pain, as near to physical death as he had ever been. In the eloquent words of Mrs. Multinerry, the organist, his face had been "… white as a ghost, Father, like as if you was already dead."

Thomas had smiled then, as he did now, remembering. Gladys Multinerry could "… talk the ears off a jack-rabbit," as her husband Jake was fond of putting it. Only the seriousness of her expression and his own weakened state had stopped his smiling as she continued her description of his experience.

"You was sayin' the mass, just like always," she'd said, eyes far-away. "I always said you was a fine one with the words, Father, the best… and next thing I see you're covered in blood, drippin' from your hands and your hair as red as any rose, and your eyes is all lit up—kind of glowing-like. It was somethin', I'm tellin' you Father. It was as though, and I mean neither blasphemy nor disrespect, as though the Christ himself had come to celebrate the mass!"

Thomas had started half from his cot at those words, for that had been his own thought—what he had felt. It had been a sharing of spirit, a communion so complete that the world had seemed dim and without light for days in the aftermath. But such thoughts were surely sinful? Surely it was wrong to feel he had been selected for any special gift? More correct to say that, in his good fortune, he had become the vessel through which a genuine miracle had been poured upon the world. He prayed now, as he had every morning and every evening since that day, to prove worthy of the honor which had been bestowed.

Far below, winding its way up the coast road from San Valencez, Thomas could see Cardinal Michaels' black sedan. He steadied his shoulders and turned his gaze one last time to the rolling waves.

Glancing up at the cathedral, magnificent in the glow of the morning sun, Father Prescott sucked in a quick breath. Haloed by the sun's radiance, a figure stood, tall and proud, looking out over the sea from a balcony window. The sight momentarily trapped his gaze, filling him with wonder. Then the figure turned and was gone, and he shook his head to clear his thoughts. He could feel Cardinal Michaels' eyes upon him, but he did not turn to acknowledge them.

The film had not been significant enough evidence, even after watching and rewinding and watching it again, even after hours of pointed questions and heated accusation. Father Thomas felt as though he'd reached judgment on earth—faced his own soul, yet it was not enough. Cardinal Michaels grew more and more angry as Father Prescott pressed his investigation and did not seem convinced that Father Thomas was a charlatan. Father Prescott, obviously, was excited, and at the same time frustrated. Thomas sensed this, yet it did nothing to allay his own fear—his own inner pain.

Nothing was resolved. Cardinal Michaels thought him a self-serving exhibitionist, albeit a clever one. Father Prescott found him enigmatic, fascinating, and had no solution to offer. The only thing they were all certain of was that there would have to be something more—something decisive. Being nearly Easter, it was fairly obvious what that would have to be.

"I will be there, firsthand," Father Prescott had assured him kindly. "Do not believe I accuse you. I seek only truth, and I truly want to help."

The cardinal's eyes had narrowed, hearing these words, but he was willing, if it put an end to what he considered a travesty, to go through with almost anything. His approval was granted, and all that awaited was the coming of Good Friday.

Shivering, Thomas went about the day-to-day duties of ministering to his parish and the church. Each task seemed more poignant, more meaningful than any day of his past. How could he face the possibility that he was unworthy, that it might not fall to him to accomplish these things any longer if Father Prescott were to determine that he was somehow to blame for what had happened.

Each reading of prayer, each mass, seemed to flow forth from some deep, inner region of his heart. He saw each parishioner with eyes rimmed in loving tears—and they noticed. It was as if they all felt it too, the culmination of their own miracle. None of them doubted him. None of them thought him less than a saint, and it buoyed his spirits, but not enough to mask the pain. Not enough to erase the fear of inadequacy. Easter had never seemed so long in coming.

Everything that happened was a slow-motion blur, surreal and hazy. People filed into the old church, filling the pews to maximum in a startlingly small amount of time. Father Prescott hovered around the perimeters of everything he did, watching, a smile of encouragement on his lips and a fiery look of determination in his eyes. Father Thomas trembled. He nearly stumbled as the time came to mount the carpeted steps beyond the altar. The weight of a thousand eyes, a weight that he'd never felt with such intensity, bore down on his shoulders. His eyes teared, but he brushed the moisture away quickly, fighting for control. He must not falter. It must be over—finished. If all he had were faith, so be it. Faith was all Saul of Tarsus had had, it was all that had been left to the earth—but it was a wondrous faith, and it would see him through.

The sacraments went with surprising fluidity. Every heart seemed to beat in unison. Every expectant face bolstered his flagging confidence. God would not mislead the multitude, he told himself. God would not let his prayers pass unanswered. And, feeling again the weakness in his knees, he prayed that God would not let him stumble, for it was painfully obvious that his own strength alone would never see him through the ordeal to come. He stepped forward, raising his arms, and it began.

Father Prescott focused on the young priest's eyes, shutting the world around him out as cleanly as if there had been shutters pulled. As clear a delineation as day and night. Cardinal Michaels became no more than a brooding darkness at his side. The multitude of parishioners surrounding him, hemming him in with the heat of their bodies and the intensity of their emotions, became the walls of a personal temple. Inside, the mass had begun, and he watched with the eyes of a hawk, watched and waited to learn.

At first, nothing seemed odd. Father Thomas began with a voice cracked and wavering, obviously near to being overcome by the sheer emotional intensity of the moment. But was it fear? Fear of being discovered, fear of being caught in clever deception, or was it an act? Was arrogance flowing so strongly through the young man's veins that he was confident his own talent would see him through a charade of such magnitude? Or—and Father Prescott's blood quickened at the thought— was the Christ working in him, and would this be the day a miracle walked the earth?

Then the words of the mass became more rhythmic, more sustained. The flow of litany and the roar of response became deafening. The words no longer mattered; it was the sound— crescendo after crescendo—verse after verse. It was almost enough to distract him from the moment. It was the most eloquent, powerful rendering of the Holy Mass he'd ever witnessed—breathtaking in its beauty. Then the blood began to show around Father Thomas' wrists, and he staggered, righting himself with a superhuman effort. The haze of emotion blotted thought from Father Prescott's mind in a numbing snap. Something was happening—something powerful—and he was a part of it. Despite his need to be as clinical and detached in his analysis as possible, it was soul-shaking.

The line of blood had formed now on Father Thomas' brow, dripping in a sticky red ring—a tiara of crimson. His arms, raised in supplication, flowed out to the sides of the pulpit— hovering in midair at shoulder height, slightly up-turned. The body sagged, as though no support remained in the legs, but it did not fall. The eyes, a symphony of pain, rolled heavenward, and the features of the young priest's face carved themselves into an image of agony beyond description. The mass continued. The voice that spoke the words cracked like thunder.

The final Divine Liturgy began, and Father Prescott fought the hold that the words had gained on his limbs, fought his emotions as they sought to make him one with the moment—with the crowd. Something was wrong. Something was happening, and he had to do something—to help the young man on the stage before it was too late. He shook his head rapidly from side to side, covered his ears with his hands so tightly that all sound should have been cut off—along with the flow of blood—but both pounded on through his mind—relentless.

He staggered to his feet, turning to look for aid from Cardinal Michaels, eyes wild. The Cardinal was oblivious to his surroundings. His face was a mask of wonder. His hands were clasped so tightly across his breast that it must have been painful. His eyes were riveted on the scene unfolding before them.

Father Prescott began stumbling blindly down the aisle, only half aware of his motions, but aware that he must hurry—that the final verses must not be spoken. He reached the altar, tried to cross the small wooden barricade and tripped, stumbling to his knees against the steps that led to the pulpit. He raised his eyes—reached upward toward where Father Thomas hung, eyes beseeching the heavens, suspended impossibly in mid-air. The mass came to an end, the words echoing endlessly through the chapel—through his mind—and still he stared.

Blood drained from Father Thomas' brow. Rivers of blood ran from the side of the priest's vestments, which were clinging, wet and brightest blood-red to his side. The spear, Father Prescott's mind screamed wildly. Father Thomas' arms, also drenched in blood, still hung from invisible supports. His legs were limp, yet he did not fall. It was too much. Blood was pooling underneath Father Prescott's knees, and his head slumped forward, mind going dark and numb with overloaded emotion. It was over. God save them all, it was over.

Cardinal Michaels sat alone in his office. The sun had long since abandoned the spring-time sky, and the church was dark, save for the single light he burned to read by. It was a large, white candle, and he held his Bible very close to the light, lips moving in silent prayer as his eyes scanned verse after verse, searching for answers.

Father Prescott had departed that morning for The Vatican. His report had already been forwarded to The Pope, endorsed by the Cardinal's own shaking hand. Father Thomas' body had been interred at a public service Friday evening—late. It had seemed best to finish things as quickly as possible—what else was there to do?

On the desk beside the candle and the Bible sat a tall glass of red wine. His third. It was growing late, but there was no sleep in his heart. No rest. He shuddered as the clock on the wall came into view, and he saw that the time was near. It was Easter, the third day since Father Thomas had died at Mass— three days since faith had become a real, tangible force to one small parish of believers. Three days since Cardinal Michaels' own faith and beliefs had been shorn of their false purity. Three days. He looked again at the clock, and he wept. He had not believed, and it was the third day—he feared what was to come. His mind slid from verse to verse, prayer to prayer, but his heart was focused.

He waited.

Yours, the Vengeance

Within six concentric circles of soaring oaks, a seventh circle began to rotate. Feet shuffled in odd rhythmic patterns, never tripping, never touching one to another. Robes flowed, catching in the wind and whipping about bare ankles. In the circle's center, alone and still as stone, she stood, eyes searching the heart of the moon—lit sky, arms uplifted in silent supplication. She was oblivious to the whirling bodies that surrounded her. She was lost in vision—caught in a fleeting moment of power. Uplifted.

Her lips parted, and a chant rose. It seemed to flow from the surrounding trees, to ride on the breeze of midnight. It echoed from the mouths of night—birds, scuttled through dry leaves and brush on quicksilver shadow—feet. It matched the dance of the others—reached out and commanded them, led them, until the chant danced among their flying feet, ethereal partner in an eerie waltz. Then it stopped. Everything stopped. The circle froze, stationary in the half—darkness. The chant grew silent, echoing through the trees. Fading.

A new sound rose. It was a sing—song, lilting melody— almost a whistle. It was joined by a harmony, and a second, a third. Each voice blended in oddly, but none was discordant. None broke the flow of sound. The woman's robes fell away, sliding to the ground and pooling at her feet. Naked, she was breathtaking. Her form was tanned and muscled, breasts proud and uplifted, shoulders strong, but not too broad. Her hair, dark in the silver light, fell past her shoulders and cascaded down the center of her back in a silken waterfall.

She reached out, grasping at the rays of moonlight as though they might suspend her in air. She breathed deeply, searching for the power, for the mother's touch. It was fleeting—less powerful than ever before. She struggled, sending all the strength of heart and mind in beseeching pursuit, grasped at the frail edges of the weakened power and pulled it to herself as if she might wrap herself in it. Her body glistened in a slick sheen of sweat. Her lovely features contorted with the effort of her call. No sound—perhaps not even a breath—escaped those who watched—who waited.

The Goddess is old, she breathed, reaching. Old as the mountains are old, strong as the wind, deep as the ocean, inevitable as the tide. I will be her servant, her bride, her vessel on the earth. I and the goddess are one! Slowly she felt the energy filling her, taking control of her limbs and filling her with new strength. Her breath came more easily, and she released herself to the wind.

The others continued their song, singing to the mother, to the earth. Her legs whipped into motion, flinging her toward the stars and catching her as she descended, infinite in grace, lost in the dance. It was a dance filled with emotion, with fleeting glimpses of power and rippling innuendos of deep— rooted faith. Her body bent and flowed like willow limbs in summer, whirled like wind in a storm. Her hair flipped about her like a whirlwind, flinging droplets of sweat to catch flickering moonlight in a prismatic, natural light show.

There was no way for her to know how long it lasted. She knew nothing when the goddess was with her. When she stopped, when all was still and she looked about to find herself alone in the clearing, the dawn was reaching tentative fingers of gold toward the sky. The trees made a beautiful, majestic silhouette against the raging morning colors—beautiful and tragic. Tears came to her then, tears of pain, and of fear. It had almost not come. The power had almost deserted her. Now it lay on her shoulders alone, the weight of redemption—of renewal. She knew what must be done, but she did not know if she had the strength to do it. She did not know if she were too late in making herself try.

As the sun rose, she walked quickly back through the trees, nearing the edge of the forest just as the first clanking roar of machinery shattered the stillness. She skirted the edge of the newly cleared area near the freeway, refusing herself the renewed pain of watching as the mechanized monsters as they ripped gaping holes in the earth. She stepped quickly around the large wooden sign that bordered the gateway to the road. It seemed to flash its message at her in bold, black print.

"Future sight of Watermania, San Valencez's newest summer attraction. Willoughby Brothers, Contractors."

She shuddered as visions of mountains of wax—covered soda cups and popcorn wrappers, choking the edges of the forest even further back, inch by inch, invaded her mind. The park would take up nearly ten acres of land that had once been protected by the state. It would cover her grove. It would cover her heart, burying it deeper in the concrete, steel, and fiberglass than she could ever hope to recover it from. She would die, as surely as the trees would die, as surely as the animals, forced deeper and deeper into forest homes grown shallower and shallower would wither and cease to exist.

The weight of responsibility was greater than she remembered. Much greater. It was one thing to become one with a long line of those sworn to protect—to defend. It was another to become the one upon whose shoulders the task actually fell. Melting back into the shadows of the trees, she moved inward, toward the forest's heart. She knew where she must go. She had not thought to go there again until it was time to pass the service to the next—until her burden would be carried by another. She prayed silently to be worthy; there would be no second chances.

———

Vines and tangled brush cloaked the cave's entrance from prying eyes. It was nearly impenetrable—as though the mother were closing in upon herself. She had not come here since that night, years before, when she'd come with that other—her predecessor. She had entered this cave, alone and frightened, young and naive. She had entered with the mother's blessing. Was that blessing still open to her? She was of the race of destroyers, after all. The same red blood flowed through her veins as through those that ran the machines, planned the destruction. She parted the vines and slid into cool, inviting darkness.

Inside, doubt seemed distant. The mother was all around her, comforting her and lending her strength. She moved through the darkness with unerring precision, though the walls of the passage were narrow and the ceiling lower than her full height. She knew what she sought, and she moved to the pool with an economy of motion, seating herself cross—legged before the stone basin and lowering her head in prayer.

She drifted closer and closer to oneness with her goddess, further and further from the ravaged earth at her back. At some point her eyes opened, and she beheld again the pool that had given her life purpose. The greenish, still expanse of the liquid swirled with inner motion. No ripple disturbed the flat, mirror—like surface, but a world—perhaps several—of visions lived in its depths.

She saw herself, much younger, kneeling at the pool, dancing in the grove. She saw others—serving in their own way. She saw the machines, rolling in and devouring earth like gargantuan insects at a predatory feast. She saw the protests—they had tried so hard to convince the men of power not to desecrate the trees. She saw Councilman Danning, the champion of Watermania, deep blue eyes smiling their reptilian smiles of greed and corruption. She saw the triumph twist the comers of his mouth as the bill passed the city and moved on through the state—as the trees lost their lives to progress.

And then the visions moved to the future... to her future. She shivered, wanting to pull away as the task before her spread itself. It was too much. Vengeance was too painful—too empty a victory. But she watched, and she trembled, and she knew she would do as she was directed. There was nothing else. The goddess was her life. Without the grove, without the trees and the dance, there was no life for her. She would answer the summons to service, though it cost her her sanity—her humanity.

The cloudy surface misted over again, becoming nothing more than a brackish pool of stagnant water. The blackness began to close around her claustrophobically. She was no longer welcome. She had her purpose, her direction, and she had so little time in which to accomplish so much. Rising, she stumbled out of the cave, banging her legs and arms—even once her head—on the cold, dank walls of the cavern. Her arms were scratched by the vines as she parted them, as though they had been ravaged by grasping claws. Tears stained her cheeks and blurred her sight.

The crowds milled about expectantly, necks stretching to the limits to take in the rising slopes of the giant slide and the small group gathered at its top. Cameramen and reporters bustled about both above and below, all focusing on the coming attraction. Danning watched them with mild amusement, standing atop the waterslide in an almost comical pair of floral print, knee-length swimming trunks. His instincts told him that the humorous approach was best; "keep 'em laughin," his father would've said. "They won't notice then if you're tryin' to trip 'em."

He stepped forward, nearly to the edge of the slide, and the master of ceremonies cleared his throat loudly through the park's PA system. The time was almost upon them, and Danning felt unnaturally nervous. He figured it must be the height.

Below, spreading through the crowd quickly, a group of green—clad spectators moved from seemingly random places in the crowd to surround the large pool at the bottom of the slide. There were five of them, and their positions formed the points of a huge pentagram. Directly across from where Danning stood, long hair blowing dreamily about her face, eyes boring through the bright sunlight in search of Danning's own, stood a woman he was certain he'd seen before, but he couldn't place her. Danning would not have noticed her, but she was raising her arms—as if in supplication. At first he'd thought she was waving... until he caught her eyes. As he moved forward to return the wave, his feet slipped clumsily. He stumbled and found himself seated at the top of the slide, slipping over the edge; falling into the steaming, accusing depths of her eyes.

It became a blurry, surrealistic kaleidoscope of sensation— slow motion and oddly focused. He could hear a strange droning sound, matched in rhythm by the movements of the woman's lips, echoed around him from all sides, caroming from invisible walls to crash back against him. It sounded like some sort of chant, but it was loud enough to drown out the PA, and that wasn't possible. He could see an ocean of upturned, expectant faces... children, women, boys and men, all focused on him, all waiting. Their mouths opened, lips moving in the patterns of cheers and laughter that Danning could somehow not hear.

His ears pounded with the rushing of the water as he slid — greased lightning on rippling waves—toward those eyes. The drone seemed to become coherent—to make sense. It was a chant, a mantra, a...

Pain! Searing, ripping pain. The world jerked crazily, throwing him to the left and slamming him impossibly into the fiberglass side of the slide. Strange pressures exerted themselves on the skin of his shoulders, his left thigh, and his back. The ocean of smiles melted to screaming, pointing demons. His eyes rolled back, searching for the fingers that gripped him. He should be at the bottom. It should be over, and he should be standing in front of WTOK's camera crew, smiling and drying off. He was not. He was suspended, caught, and...

He screamed when the sight of the first hook, ripping a bloody trench through his shoulder, came into view. His mind numbed like a lake freezing in winter, emptying of thought before it could erode sanity. His body twitched and convulsed. Sickening, tearing sounds erupted from his back, from his legs. His mind snapped, and his eyes rolled sideways, tracing the trail of the water. Trickling red ribbons took the path meant for him, completing his journey. As all hell broke loose below, the blood reached the pool.

She stood now on the edge of the huge basin, eyes upraised,

arms reaching toward the sky. Her lips never faltered. Her eyes slowly closed, erasing the world and locking her in. The eyes of every man, woman, and child around her were locked on the twirling, dangling figure of Councilman Chuck Darning. His floral shorts seemed to have turned to crimson. His movements, as long as they lasted, were those of an oddly clumsy puppet. Nobody noticed her; not at first.

The others had stepped up to the pool's edge as well. Their movements mirrored hers. Their arms reached, their voices rose. They could be heard beneath the screams of the crowd — their chant. It was primal, blending to the fear around them and magnifying it.

Dying, Chuck Danning heard it clearly — exclusively. As his blood swirled to the bottom, his mind swirled to darkness. He felt cold — cold in spite of the beating rays of the sun — colder than he'd ever been.

Below, the water had darkened, changed hue. It could not be only his blood. The chant went on. He wanted to raise his eyes a final time, to gaze into her eyes and to ask, "Why?" — but it was denied him. His body would not obey — it seemed dislocated — detached. All he could do was to watch the blood, to listen to the chant as it droned on, to die… slowly.

Would — be heroes were already making their way up service ladders, but it was far too late. The weight of his body, aided by the pummeling force of the water that poured down the slide, had seen to that. Ripping great gashes in his skin, feeding his blood to the pool. The dark pool, so like her eyes, so strangely powerful… so dark… so cold. So…

It was done. The blood had flowed. The sacrifice lay dead, flayed alive on the altar of his greed. Beneath her she could feel the goddess, flowing through the water, tracing the patterns of power, flowing up from the force lines beneath the now desecrated grove. She hungered. The goddess hungered. The grove screamed to be renewed—reborn. Some around her were now aware that something was wrong—beyond the dead fool on the slide—that something was happening in the pool. It did not matter. Even were she to die on the spot, the result would be the same. The ritual was complete. The waters rolled, swirled, a maelstrom of shifting shapes and rippling power. Turning, she moved quickly toward the forest. She would watch, but she would do so from a distance. She knew only too well the wrath of her goddess... a wrath not unleashed in centuries—a madness that would consume all in its path, cleansing where man had desecrated.

As the woman and her followers melted to the shadows of the forest, the water began to rise, chasing its shadow on the screaming, running crowds. A foolish newsman, camera in hand, stood filming it as it rose. He was dashed to pulp by the fist slap of wave—fingers on earth. The walls of the pool gave way then, and the power flooded outward, wiping the land clean, clearing the debris, destroying Watermania as though it had never existed.

As the park crumbled, and those in the very fringe of the crowd made their escape, staring with fear—maddened eyes at the huge, glaring countenance rising in waves of pure water above them, Councilman Danning's body finally lost the war with gravity. As the slide crumbled, his inert form went tumbling downward, finally making the journey toward the pool below. The elemental turned, as though just noticing him. Those that saw swear it turned and opened its arms, awaiting him with a cold embrace.

It took many years, but the trees began to grow.

On the Road to Damascus

Saul kept the bundle of letters beneath his tunic, pressed against his breast where he could feel the roughness of the parchment scratching against his skin as he walked. The pain was a constant reminder of his mission, of the grand task set before him. He would find them, all those who followed the "way" of Jesus of Nazareth, all of those who believed that this man had been more than just a man—more even than a prophet.

Their eyes had been dimmed, their thoughts clouded. The scriptures talked of a Messiah, it was true, but years of study had instilled in Saul a burning passion for those prophecies, knowledge of scripture and history that few were blessed with, and he knew better. He felt within himself a purpose, a destiny that would not allow him to believe the true "Christ" had come to the Earth and he'd had no part in it.

It was not the Christ they followed, he told himself, but the thought of the Christ. They saw suffering, they saw problems they did not believe they could overcome through faith and scripture alone, and they followed whoever would lead. The true leadership, that of the priests and the temples, was a narrow, difficult path—a path only for the strong of heart. They could hardly be blamed for choosing a simpler, easier way, but they had to learn their error.

That this Jesus had been a powerful, perhaps even a great man was not in doubt. Saul knew well enough about control, about the nature of the masses. Jesus had known as well, had in fact been a master of such power. Saul's own mission was all about control, his own control, his future. He would go, leading his small army to the synagogues and temples and routing the followers of this upstart from Nazareth, and his own place in the temple would be secure. He would be lauded as a prophet himself, a man of vision—a warrior of the Lord.

As the sun began to set, leaving them one short day's journey from Damascus, he raised his hand to signal a halt and led his followers to the side of the road. There was no sense in going on in the darkness, and they were close enough, in any case, to reach their journey before the afternoon sun got too hot on the following day.

As he turned to give instructions, he was engulfed. The light rose with stunning quickness, like lightning, or the sudden glare of the sun from the tips of waves along the shore. It filled his sight, then his mind, brushing aside thought and sanity with the contemptuous indifference of the omnipotent.

Saul raised his hands to his eyes, and then slid them around to press tightly against the sides of his head as agony ripped through him, driving him to his knees. In the span of an instant, his mind was emptied, then refilled. Where thought had been was pain, where control had lingered, fire.

He screamed incoherently, dropping so that his forehead was pressed into the hot sand, beating mindlessly on the ground with his fists, then bringing them back to his head and pounding on his temples, as though he might drive the pain physically from himself. Still the light pulsed through him, robbing him of his strength, emptying him of all but pain.

He lay still, the tortuous burning fire slamming through his veins for what seemed hours, days, perhaps, giving himself over at last to the helplessness of the situation, waiting for it to end. Finally, as he felt himself drifting away, or the light receding, thought began to slip back through his muddled senses. He could hear frightened voices, could feel hands upon his shoulders, could feel the heat of the sand and smell the sweat of others nearby—very near. It was still jumbled, still confused, but it was a comfortable confusion, a familiar jumble.

Rising shakily, he pulled his hands away from his head, and he opened his eyes. Vertigo latched onto his senses again, and he nearly retched as it sent him reeling back to the Earth. There was nothing. Black, empty, nothingness. He could still hear, could hear them babbling his name, asking foolish questions, but he could see nothing. He rubbed his eyes furiously, shutting them and opening them again with a snap, repeating the motions rapidly. Nothing. Blind.

"I am blind." he said simply, trying to rise and stumbling, having no balance—no way to find his bearings. He felt hands clutching at him, grabbing beneath his armpits clumsily, but even with their help he failed to find his feet.

He was trembling now, sweat pouring from him in small, dusty rivers and leaving him cold inside. Blind. What had the light been? What could it mean? And where had his world gone?

He tried to rise again, failed, and finally he sat back on his heels, his head turned to the heavens where he could still feel the sun beating down upon him, where his mind told him that the sky was still blue, though the color was fast losing clarity in his memory.

His eyes were open wide—he could feel the burning glare against them, could feel the pain that this should cause, but there was no glare in his mind. There was no glimmer; no lightening of the darkness tempered the void. Empty. Blind.

Then he felt a voice begin to insinuate itself through his thoughts. At first he could not distinguish it from the voices of the others around him, the babbling, nonsensical words of fear and worry that his followers continued to batter him with, despite his attempts to wave them aside, to silence them.

Then things changed. The world around him faded, the sounds fell away, the smells and the heat of the sun faded, and within the void the sound of that single, disembodied voice clarified, wiping all other images from his mind, wiping out the memory of the sand beneath him and the sun on his skin, wiping out all that had been his world and supplanting it easily.

He felt himself floating, adrift in blackness so total, so incredibly empty, that his only significance was that, for that moment in time, he was. Nothing else existed, only his body, which he could still sense, could still reach out with his hands and touch, and the voice, growing in strength and filling him from within—forcing him to listen, and to understand. It named him, and in that naming, saved him from dissolution.

Saul, the voice called to him, Saul, why are you persecuting me this way?

"Who are you?" he cried. "What have you done—what have I done?" He felt the breath leaving him, felt the vibration of the sound within him, but there was nothing. He wasn't certain if he'd made a noise, if he would be heard.

You know me, Saul of Tarsus, though your heart will not admit it. I have done many works in the land, things of which you have heard and disbelieved. My followers are many, and yet you show them no compassion.

"You are Jesus, then." he called out loudly, naming his enemy. It did not give him comfort, but somehow it made things more real—more solid. "What shall I do, Lord? What would you have of me?"

You must arise, Saul of Tarsus, and go into Damascus. There you will await my summons, and you will be told what to do.

The voice was gone then. It did not fade, did not slide away as it had taken him but snapped out of existence with a suddenness that left him short of breath and trembling. He felt the difference, knew that, somehow, he was back on his knees, back in the sand beside the road to Damascus. The heat was lessened, the sun setting, and yet it was still day. All of this he registered in the span of a few seconds. Then, remembering those around him, he cried out to them.

"What have you seen?" he demanded loudly, "What have you heard?"

"We... we heard a voice, Saul," one of his followers, a man named Joseph, said shakily. "There was a whirling of sand, and a voice, talking in tones too low for us to hear, yet there was nobody there. We heard you, as well, heard you crying out to someone. What has happened, Saul? What shall we do?

He tried to clear his mind. Confusion battered at his thoughts each time he tried to order them, but he bulled his way through, forcing himself to make sense of it. They were counting on him, counting on him to show them the way, to interpret the sign. He was without sight, but he did not know for how long, and he had been chosen. This meant, somehow, that he had the strength to pull himself through.

That his purpose was changed could not be doubted. He was schooled in the ways of the temple, well-read in the scriptures, and he was no fool. When a genuine miracle presented itself, singling him out from a crowd, he knew it to be a good thing—a sign of favor. In some way, though he was the worst of the Christ's enemies, he had been chosen.

"We must move on," he said at last. "You must help me to rise, this very hour, and we must continue on to the city. I have been given a sign, but my sight has been taken from me. You must lead me, and I must think on what I have seen, what I have heard. When we reach the city, there we will find our answers."

They were not pleased about traveling on that night, but they were content to follow his lead, as he'd known they would be. After a few moments of haggling and shuffling about of the baggage, they managed to free up a man to aid Saul along the way, and they set out once more for Damascus.

Along the road, shadows danced as the sun set and the moon replaced it in the sky. Colors washed the sky, outlining the clouds in silver and smoky red, but Saul saw none of it. Later, though, when the moon had fully ascended her throne and the cooler breeze of night wound through his hair, he would have sworn that he could feel the soft luminescence brushing over him as well. It was a night of wonders.

———

They made it into the city without further incident, and they made their way directly to the house of a man named Judas, who was expecting them. Saul gave no explanation for his situation. He handed over his letters, distractedly, and then he asked to be taken to a room, alone, and to be left. Within, he waited, taking no food or water, fasting as he sat his lonely vigil.

The voice had told him to come to the city and to wait, and that was what he did. Being a man of strong passion, he did nothing half way. If he were going to wait for a holy vision, well, he knew only too well how to go about that. He cleansed himself. The scriptures had a ritual for every occasion, advice for every dilemma. All that was necessary was to read, to understand, and to remember.

Already he'd begun to see the loss of his sight as a blessing, an aid to his meditation and preparation. He had been stripped of the distractions of the world about him. This allowed him to focus his thoughts, as did the hunger, and the thirst.

He spoke to no man, nor did they press him. All in the house gave the room where he sat a wide berth, not knowing if he were possessed, mad, or blessed. He waited there for three days, and on the third day—as it had been in Jerusalem—as if it were a sign, he was summoned.

There was a knock on the door below, and outside stood a man of the city, a man named Ananias. He claimed to have been visited by a spirit, an angel that had sent him to that very house to see Saul of Tarsus.

As he stood before Judas, he trembled, sweat running down his face and under his tunic in small rivulets. The fear in his eyes was nearly a tangible force. Ananias was one of the faithful, a Christian, and he knew well enough who Saul was—what his mission was to be. The letters had been spread about through the temples the night the group had arrived.

Still, in faith, he had come, and he was admitted immediately and led to where Saul sat alone in his room. Though those present knew him as well, and where his faith was invested, they chose not to interfere.

"Saul," Ananias said softly, "Can you hear me?"

"I am blind, not deaf," Saul replied shakily. "What is it that you want? Who are you, and why are you here?"

"You have met my Lord on the road to Damascus, Saul, and he has come to me as well, appearing as a voice from within a great, pure light. He sent me to you that you might have your sight returned, and that you might be filled with the Holy Spirit."

"You are to heal me?" Saul asked, confused.

"No, I am to bring you to the oracle. There you will be healed, and there you will find the answers you seek. Will you come with me?"

There was strangeness in the air, an air of anticipation, of powers on the move. Saul felt it, and he wasn't certain how to interpret it. Ananias felt it, as well, and he quaked inside. It did not have the same feel as the spirit he shared with his brothers, with those of the "Way." It was darker, more urgent, and more insistent.

Still, he had seen a vision—a blinding light—heard voices in his head where there should have been nothing, speaking to him and instructing him. Saul had seen that light as well, had been blinded by it, and if it was up to Ananias to bring this man to the "Way," he would sacrifice all that he was to do so.

"I will come," Saul said at last, holding out his hand for Ananias to help him rise. "I do not know what is expected of me, but I have seen a sign. I will do what your Lord—our Lord—directs."

Ananias nodded. Then, feeling foolish for nodding to a blind man, he took the hand that was offered and helped Saul to stand, leading him to the doorway and down to the lower level of the house.

"Where do you go, Saul?" Joseph asked anxiously. "Has your sight not been returned?"

"In time, Joseph, in time," Saul assured his friend wearily. "I am weakened, but there is still more required of me, it seems. I will leave with this man for a short time, and I will return when I have found that which I seek. Await me here, and I will bring you that answer; this I swear."

He heard them shuffling about, heard them whispering among themselves and arguing in hushed voices, but he paid them no further heed. They could believe, or not, follow or do as they pleased. They had not heard the voice—they had not been blinded by the light of the Lord. They were not chosen, and if his path and theirs were to part, so be it.

Turning, he allowed Ananias to lead him out into the street and away, letting the voices of his followers die away behind them. It was not about them, not really. They were with him. What had happened was his alone, at least until he'd made enough sense of it to get the full impact straight in his mind. He could not share a message he had not fully received.

As they moved through the city he noticed the odd clarity that the lack of his sight gave to his other senses. He could pick out sounds, scents that would have eluded him previously, or been filtered out by his thoughts and his vision. Food smelled somehow better—though that could also have had something to do with his three-day fast.

He could tell a woman's voice from a child's, a young man's from an old man's, could even tell from the sound of their footsteps if they were small or large, crippled or in a hurry. It was a small revelation, a minor miracle within the framework of a larger one. He tucked each tidbit away for later use, recorded each thought carefully against the trials that were to come.

It was a long walk, carrying them through the center of the city and beyond it, into the hills. The oracle was a famous place, spoken of in whispers among Jews and Christians alike, still attended by the odd Roman, or those with questions they thought the world might not answer for them. It was a shadowed place, and it was this that made Saul uneasy as he walked.

Why would the Messiah choose such a place to make his will known? Why the theatrics? If he wanted something, Saul was ready to deliver it, more than ready. His entire life he'd believed himself destined for greatness. They'd told him as much in the temple, seeing his aptitude for the scriptures and hearing the quickness of his tongue.

He was a man destined for great things, and yet he knew his place. If the Christ had indeed walked the Earth, if Saul and all his brothers at the temple had been wrong, then he would shoulder the associated guilt and he would set about making things right. What else could he do?

Ananias seemed content to walk in silence, and Saul wondered what the man might be thinking. He knew the man was a Christian, that he was aware of why he had come to Damascus, and it was obvious that he was afraid. His steps were nervous, furtive, even, and yet he had shown great courage, amazing faith, to come as he had been directed, walking trustingly into the house of one who had only days earlier sought his death and those of everyone he held dear.

Saul would have liked to have questioned him, to have tried to glean for himself some understanding of what had given him his faith, what power motivated his thoughts. He wanted very much to know more than he did of the man, Jesus, and what had transpired in Jerusalem. He wanted to know, but he kept his silence.

He still had no idea what he was destined for. It was possible that he was only being brought here to be silenced, to be made an example of. His was a vengeful God, and if Jesus of Nazareth had truly been that God, made flesh and set upon the Earth, would he be more compassionate now?

He felt Ananias hesitate, and some inner sense told him that they neared their goal. The other man's hesitance reminded him of his own questions about the place. He wished that he had his eyes, and that he could see clearly what it was that he was getting himself into.

"Tell me of this oracle," he said softly. "Tell me what it looks like, who is here? I cannot understand why I have been summoned here, though I come gladly."

"I do not know the answer," Ananias answered. "You must only believe, Saul, and he will come to you. Faith is our support; his love is our salvation. If you believe that, no darkness can touch you.

"This place is like a cavern, though there are torches lighting the way inside—I can see them even from here. There are no others. We passed one woman, very dark-eyed and staring, on the road a ways back, but she hurried toward the city when she saw us. We are alone."

Saul felt his heartbeat quickening, small bumps of fear bristling on his arms and running up his spine like pincers of ice. Squaring his shoulders, he urged Ananias forward again.

"Did your vision show you what I must do here?" he whispered as they moved on.

"No." Ananias answered. "The voice told me only that I must bring you inside the cave, before the oracle, and that I am to await you outside."

"Then let us go to him," Saul said, striding forward purposefully. "Let us find the answers."

———

Anananias left him, seated cross-legged in a cool, damp place. There was a slight breeze coming from somewhere behind him, from the cave's entrance, he was thought, if his directions were not totally skewed, being sucked into some inner chamber, or tunnel in the mountain. There was the sound of running water as well, the echo of each drop caroming about and resonating from the walls.

Ananias had disappeared from his side what seemed eternities earlier, and yet he had neither heard the voice returning, nor been granted a vision. His skin had chilled, and the hunger rumbled in his stomach, and still he sat, eyes pointed forward—seeing nothing—empty. He fought to maintain his faith, his concentration, refusing to give in to doubt.

He was never certain later if the cold or the sound penetrated his mind first. The room had become like ice, freezing the blood in his veins and setting his teeth to chattering incessantly. He held himself upright with a great effort, ignoring the cold as best he could, and eventually it receded from his heart. It was then that he realized that he could make out words, echoing through his mind and suddenly untangling themselves from the confusion that bound his thoughts.

Saul. The voice was the same, though more sibilant, more powerful—darker somehow. Saul, you have come, and this is good. Why do you believe that I have brought you here?

"I do not know, Lord," he stammered, fighting the cold to force the words past his lips. "I have persecuted you throughout the land... and this is a strange place for instruction."

You believe then that I am Jesus? He heard then what might have been a rumble within the Earth, or laughter—deep, mocking laughter. Now his fear was doubled—had he made a mistake? Was he to become possessed?

It is good that you believed as you did, the voice went on, but I am not what you think. I am sent as a guide, sent by the All-Father in Heaven to set your feet on the proper path.

You are learned in the scriptures, Saul, and your ardor and zeal are not unknown to your God. You have moved across the land as an avenging angel, purging the followers of this upstart "messiah" with confidence and purity.

It is not enough, though. They multiply, even as you put them to death. Every one you purge becomes yet another martyr to their cause. Every time you move to cleanse their hearts and minds, those who remain twist your words and deeds in ways that bring more under their influence.

Saul was shaking. He did not know with whom he spoke, but it was obviously not Jesus, as he had supposed. His sight was gone, and for that moment, he was glad—glad that whatever entity belonged to that overly-sweet, heart-rendingly seductive voice, was not holding his eyes within its own, and delving into his soul.

You must go to them, Saul, and they must believe that you have seen the Christ. You must gain their trust, accepting their meaningless baptism and preaching their words in the temples. You must convince them that you are the most devout of their number, and you must destroy them from within.

It is a great task I set before you, Saul, a sacrifice beyond that asked of any other. When you have their trust, you can twist their faith.

You understand control. I can see it in your heart, can feel it in your words and deeds. You can control them, Saul of Tarsus, and you can bring about their fall much more completely, much more totally, from within.

Give them rules. Men love rules. Give them points to argue over, points that will distract them from the central tenets of their faith. You have argued the scriptures with the best; you know what will give them the most difficulty. Give them rules to break, and they will be stoning one another within the year.

You will be my new-world tower of Babel, Saul. You will take their one church and confuse its teaching so that it breaks off into a multitude of smaller, less powerful faiths. When you have accomplished this, the one true temple will shine forth once more, as it has since the creation, lighting the way for the day when the Messiah truly comes.

They are an iniquitous lot, impatient and arrogant. They believe that a few good works and fine words can bring prophecy to life. You understand prophecy better than any man alive, and I tell you, you can use that knowledge.

If you love me, Saul, give me your life.

Saul sat, stunned to silence by the words, by the import of their message. He had not been wrong, had not been singled out for his treachery against any true church. He was being rewarded, being granted the chance to be an instrument of the Lord's vengeance, a messenger, though clandestinely, of the One True God.

It was beyond his hopes, beyond his dreams. He leaned forward, kneeling and dropping his head to the icy stone. His hands and feet were growing numb, and his head felt light—dizzy from the exertion of his walk and the lack of food. It did not affect his clarity of vision at that moment, did not distract him from the wonder of the glory that was bestowed upon him.

"I will do as you ask, Lord," he said, knowing that his words were not necessary, that his intentions and his purity would be read in his heart and mind. "I will go to them, and I will be their strongest—their brightest. I know the scriptures; I can argue their side as well as the truth."

It is well.

The voice and the cold disappeared with a suddenness that sucked the breath from Saul's body, leaving him heaving and panting for breath on the cavern's floor. He felt the stone, cool now, not cold, felt the dampness, and lifting his head, he felt an odd weight slipping from his eyes. He heard something clatter to the stone, but the sound was lost in the wonder of the moment.

He looked about himself, seeing that he was kneeling before a small pool, formed of water dripping from some inner source within the mountain. There were torches all about him, attempting to keep the darkness of the mountain at bay, but all they did was to accentuate the shadows of the place, to make them stand out, stark and ethereal.

He glanced down, and he saw what it was that had robbed him of his sight. Lying on the ground between his knees were two small disks, hard as stone and opaque. He lifted one, holding it up to the torchlight, and he marveled at it. It was a scale, like that of some great serpent.

He picked both scales from the ground carefully and tossed them into the pool of the oracle, watching as they disappeared into the tranquil depths. His body was still weak, and he had trouble rising, but his eyes were shining with a brightness they had never known, strength of purpose that emanated from him like a beacon. Chosen.

He left the cavern, returning to Ananias' side, and the other man fell back a step, gazing at him in wonder. Letting the light shine from within him, Saul opened his arms to the younger man and took him into a warm embrace.

"He has come to me," he said simply, "and I can see. Come, brother, we have much to do, many things to accomplish. I must eat and regain my strength."

His heart near to bursting with the joy and amazement that filled him, Ananias did as Saul instructed him, turning back to the road and setting out toward Damascus at a brisk pace.

Behind them, staring from the depths of the darkness, a pair of eyes watched with a mixture of glee and insanity, a blending of power and shadow. Angel of Light. Great serpent. With a burst of laughter that shook the very foundations of the mountain, he was gone, leaving his newest disciple to carry on. In the heavens, the angels wept.

Sparkling Eyes

The water sparkled like a million diamonds, multi-faceted and beautiful. Sea birds chased one another across the cloudless Vancouver sky, playing tag among craggy mountain peaks and diving to pluck their meals from the azure waves. A gentle wind played at the graying strands of his hair as he stood, a bent and aged silhouette against a backdrop of sunlight and vitality. Like the mountains, he was worn-his features creased and chiseled. Time had not been unkind, only persistent.

The years of his life were etched deeply. His eyes were a deep, dark brown—the youngest things about him. They were almost startling in their clarity and intensity. At the moment, they were trained outward, across the pounding surf and the cresting foam. Several others passed his lonely vantage point, perched on a rocky outcropping, but he did not turn to greet them, or to note their passing. He watched, back stiff, hands in the pockets of his thin, canvas jacket, until the first sleek, dark shape cleared the water's surface. They had come He counted back the years to the last time he'd seen them—further back— to the first time he'd stood on the cliffs overlooking this bay. He could almost taste her scent in the air, sweet—strawberries and summer breeze. He could hear, deep in the tinkling of salts pray on the shore, the soft, bell-like notes of her laughter. The ache had softened over the years, but it remained, a part of him that would never really heal. He smiled faintly as the familiar icy teeth sank into his heart.

There were five dark shapes now, flowing one over the other and back, endless grace driven by awesome power. He strained, searching each shape, but the distance was too great. His sight was not strong. Mildly disappointed, but not deterred, he turned slowly away, eyes shifting to the ground. He did not want scenery, even scenery that sprang as vividly from his past as it did from the present; he wanted his past. As he trudged wearily back down the trail that would lead him to the shoreline, his mind slipped past the nets of time, pulling her image back to him across years, yearning for her smile.

"Look," she said, eyes glittering with barely contained delight. "Look, David, they're coming!"

He had looked as the small band of orca cut the waves, slicing salt spray loose to shoot heavenward in prismatic fountains of light. His eyes had wandered back to hers. Had sought the glowing light of her smile. He had had to force his gaze back to the sea. Tears had formed, then, seeing her happiness, which he had quickly brushed away, that much more salt spray on the breeze.

They had come to Vancouver Island for their honeymoon. The visit was the answer to a long-past promise. The answer to her dream. David had always wanted to be the one to make those dreams reality, to be deserving of her love, and her smiles. It had been a long time in coming, that moment. It had been worth the work, worth the wait. The tears were very stubborn; he had to turn his head. The very first gift he'd ever given her had been a small, silver dolphin wrapped around a crystal of clear quartz. She loved dolphins—and whales. Her walls and shelves were lined with their images, statues, paintings—even a small mobile formed of diving dolphins was hung above the desk they'd shared. And there had been the dreams.

He'd always promised that someday, when there was money, when there was time, he'd take her to the island, to the whales. It had seemed a fantasy, especially to her. Of course she'd appreciated his thoughts, but she'd never truly believed he would make them reality. Then the book had sold. It was so much like a dream, the sudden money, the freedom, that he'd known there was only one perfect way to celebrate it. He had given her dream to her, as well.

He knew that it had been her support that had brought him to the end of writing the book, and beyond, through the endless submissions and rejections and revisions, until that magic day when his agent had called with dollar signs dripping from his voice.

Even after she left, the endless nights he spent staring into the single cyclopic eye of his computer screen and writing, trying to erase the pain of her going, her spirit had moved him. Without the depth of emotion brought by his pain, he would never have sold another word. Might never have written anything worthwhile. He owed her every minute of his life past their first kiss. It was then that he'd lost his heart, placing it trustingly in her hands, though she never promised to protect it. In fact, her words, her eyes, even her restless movements as she lay sleeping—he watching, she dreaming—had warned him not to hold on too tightly. It had been far too late to consider slowing his emotions, or slopping, but she had not promised him her life, just because he felt he had to offer her his. She just didn't know how that glittering sparkle in her eye filled his soul with love—didn't see how deeply each word she spoke effected its magic on him.

Now she was gone. They'd written—such letters as ancient poets were famous for—sharing over miles and distance things they'd lost the chance to find together.

He'd gone on to write dozens of novels, stories—some for her, a few for others. She'd read them, buying magazines when he forgot to send her copies, praising his work. And she'd told him of her loves, her problems, the growing old of her children, who he'd known only briefly, but remembered so vividly. He had no children of his own, but he held no regrets. There was life enough in the world, and he had made his contributions.

But now she was gone.

It had been only a short note, a condescending sentiment to a doddering old man from her family. They knew of him, of course, and they had known he would need to hear of her death. In fact, bad blood enough lay between them that they had probably taken a perverse pleasure in informing him of it. Probably, they would have liked to have seen the tears in his eyes, to savor the pain their news brought. He was not sorry that they were thousands of miles away.

And now, here he was, alone and los1 in memories of love so far past that for most men they would have been ashes on forgotten campfires. He was walking again in footsteps of days when his eyes had sparkled with love, and with delight at the wonders around him. Here he was trying to recapture—what? What was it he really sought?

"If I were gone," she'd said, eyes deep and serious, endearing, "you could come here." She had turned to the side of the boat they'd ridden on, leaning over the railing for a better view of the sleek, black and white forms sailing along at their side. "Part of me will never leave this place," she said wistfully. Her arm had wrapped tightly around his shoulders, pulling him closer. "I will swim with them in my dreams. They are so wonderful—and you gave them to me. When you and they are together, a part of me will always be there, too. I love you."

And he knew that she had loved him. It was different for her. He had loved so deeply, and so quickly, that she had felt smothered. It was not only in her dreams that she swam with the free-spirited. She bubbled with emotion, and she needed to be near those with energy to match her own. He had needed someone to be there, someone he could lean on in turn. That was more of a burden than she'd been willing to commit to, in the end.

He knew that his age had been a factor, as well. He was ten years older than her, caught in the webs of responsibility that life eventually wraps around all of us. He had not had the patience to wait for her to settle down, and she had not been able to curb the desire for freedom, not even for love.

He reached the bottom of the winding trail, coming to the edge of the rocky beach and into bright sunlight. The shore was covered with worn, smooth stones. Littered with them. He knew that the whales would come here, seeking the stones and rolling their great, sleek, muscled bodies over them, massaging away thousands of miles of water he could only imagine—miles they traveled on a whim. He walked until he found a comfortable seat, perched on a huge, rounded boulder, and watched as they rolled in, a moving wall of life—a vision from his own past.

What had they lived since then? He found that, in some way, he felt a link with these huge water-bound mammals that would not release him. His own miles had been littered with strife, and anger, and with the magic of words that had made him a part of lives he knew nothing of. People read his books—that had always been his dream.

His words made them cry, he supposed, or laugh—or maybe not, but they at least made them listen. Even if they all laughed and called him a fool, they read the books. He had made a difference.

Yet he had not had the slightest effect on these great, silent sharers in his life. Grand, proud, mysterious, they had gone about their solitary business. Somehow the secret lay in this, the very consistency of their reality. They were a part of his heart—as she had been a pan of his heart—and they were unchanged. They were solid, real, and they were as immovable and stolid in their existence as mountains. He knew that he had come here seeking something lost—and now he felt, inexplicably, that things had changed.

He felt as though what he was seeking had never been lost, had never changed.

It was he who had been lost, her words and these huge, natural philosophers, were helping him to find his way home. They frolicked on the beach in such a childish, immature fashion that it made him smile. They, whose strength and power could send a boat bubbling slowly to the bottom of the ocean, or face off the most violent predators that the oceans could offer up, had not lost their joy in life. They were not so serious and solemn that freedom and joy were beneath them. They did as they pleased, always.

Even as he smiled, he remembered her eyes, sparkling with joy and nearly blinding him with their light, and he could imagine her, proud and young, twining her lithe form among the larger, more ancient creatures he watched. He could imagine that she was one with them, and tears trickled down to salt his lips, even as he felt laughter bursting to the surface. It had been a long time since thoughts of her could make him laugh.

In a daze he rose, stumbling away from the beach and back toward the small cabin he had rented. His mind whirled with conflicting thoughts and images. His eyes burned from the salt of tears, whipped against them by the chill breeze of the beach. Why couldn't he let go? What was it he'd expected to find? He could have remembered her without this—without the rising ache of knowing she was lost to him—lost to her whales and to the soaring gulls. What did he think he'd find? It was late night before he finally cried himself to sleep, feeling very alone and very fragile.

Time was a heavy weight on his shoulders, and they seemed to have lost the strength of the years. The pier was much the same as it had been. Boats, small and large, dotted the length of it, some commercial, and some private. It was a hodge-podge of color and activity. He knew that the chances of the same boat being there were slim, but he couldn't help searching the length of the old pier, just in case. His eyes halted on a new, trim schooner near the far end on the left. It was not his boat—their boat—but something made him walk out and glance down at the name emblazoned across the back of it.

The Eternity, it said in bold, black letters. His eyes widened, and he looked about for the captain. It was not the same boat, true. It was brand new, paint gleaming in the sunlight and bright-work polished to a brilliant sheen. It was the name; The Eternity was the boat they'd taken so many years past—a smaller, thriftier version. He wondered if old Captain Weathers was about. Could it be? The sign by the brow read, "Chartered tours, Antonio Weatherby, Proprietor." Antonio? It had been Arturo, and… .

"Can I help you, sir?" It was a young, swarthy sailor who had spoken, rounding the corner of the small ship's cabin. He was tall, browned by the sun and weathered by salt and wind. His eyes shone with a friendly light. He was the very image of his father.

"I want to go out," David spoke finally. "I… I rode your father's vessel many, many years ago. It was a very special trip.

I just want to go out and to see the whales..." Light seemed to beam from the young man's smile. "We go again in less than an hour, sir. I'm sure my father would be flattered, was he about. He doesn't leave the house much these days. Perhaps, after we sail, you might stop by and visit? I'm sure he'd be honored to be remembered. "

"I may, at that," David smiled back. His mind seemed to tilt, to snap from one world to the next, as he mounted the small walkway and boarded The Eternity. He almost turned, almost held out his arm to steady her as she followed. There was only air, and he glanced about quickly to be certain no one had witnessed his odd slip.

Trembling, he made his way to a wooden seat along one rail to await their departure. His eyes never left the water below, even when others began to close in beside him. A young couple shared his bench, at the last moment, and he moved to one side to allow them plenty of room.

The girl's hair was red, long and shining, just as hers had been, and there was a sparkle in both the youngster's eyes that brought a tingle to his spine. His stomach noted with only the slightest queasiness the departure of the boat from the pier. A small loudspeaker began to announce the sights they would pass and to welcome them all—and the voice was so much that of the father that he could have closed his eyes and been there, so many years past.

They cut through the waves at a good clip, water splitting to the sides in a gigantic "v." They passed small villages to right and left as they departed the bay, ruins of older times, monuments to the future.

All of it was much as it had been, a bit more worn, a bit more developed in other spots, but mostly the same. He flew through it in a thick cloud of memory. Vaguely he was aware of the ample beside him, but even their words, small endearments

101

and gasps of wonder and fascination, seemed to weave themselves into the tapestry of the past he sought so desperately. They became players in a one act script from out of time, and the miles slipped beneath the boat with the rapidity of dying years.

He never knew when they reached the point—the turn-off to the open ocean—the culmination of his journey. He heard the voice describing the whales as they sliced the water, was already watching them when the words finally cut into his thoughts. They were diving and jumping, sliding one over the other in a dance of ancient intelligence and infinite grace. He was captivated.

"Oh," he heard the girl at his side gasp. "They're so beautiful!"

Yes, he thought, they are beautiful.

The girl was beautiful, too. He wanted to turn to the young man beside him, to explain to him about keeping a strong hold on his dreams, and on his happiness. He wanted to tell them to photograph this moment in their minds, that it might be the memory that bound their lives, past to present. He could not. He couldn't even turn his eyes to the side, away from the shifting panorama of strength and beauty flowing effortlessly beside the manmade craft—mocking its inadequacy, mocking his own inadequacy.

They had shared their gift of freedom and beauty with him, and he had forgotten them. He had cast aside the things that mattered most in a selfish bid for control of things he was never meant to control.

Then it happened. It was as if time slowed—sliding to a slow, coasting halt. A huge, glistening form turned, leaping through the air to crash against the water directly in front of him, spraying him and the boat with a huge wave of salt water.

Then it rose again, seeming to hover for a second in mid-air, laughing at him.

But it was the eyes that caught at him, that pinioned him to his chair and clutching at his heart. They were sea-green, bright with life, and glistening with captured sunlight. He looked — deeper than he'd ever looked into any other set of eyes but one — and he felt love — understanding. He staggered to his feet, reached out toward the warmth of those brilliant, sparkling eyes, and felt the arms closing tightly about him, the vision fading. Darkness claimed him in seconds, warm, wet, silent, and he dreamed. In his dreams, she held him tightly, soothing his cares — erasing the years of pain.

The water sparkled like a million diamonds, multi-faceted and beautiful. Sea birds chased one another across the cloudless Vancouver sky, playing tag among the craggy mountain peaks and diving to pluck their meals from the azure waves. Seated far above — a crystal goblet of wine clutched tightly in gnarled, time-worn hands, David sat, watching.

His smile was deep — deeper than the blue of the skies — deeper than the caressing limitless expanse of the ocean below. He knew that he'd come close to losing his own life to those waves — to sacrificing the one thing she would have wanted him to cherish for a moment of what — faded past? No, not faded, sparkling and golden — sea green and smiling. He had not seen at first, had not understood.

They had hauled him back over the side, the young couple and Captain Weatherby, Jr., throwing cold, fresh water on his time-worn face and holding him still as he struggled. It had only been much later, alone in his small cabin and dreaming fitfully, when he had understood.

Once again he'd tried to grab and hold what he should merely have seen and loved. He had been granted another chance, a very late blooming license on freedom. And no matter where it led him, no matter if he spent the rest of his life watching and waiting on this solitary cliff, or writing in the confines of some small condo in Sacramento—she would be with him. The memory of her eyes, the warmth of her smile— they no longer haunted him. They were his support, and his vision. He knew now that, when his time was finished, it would not be an ending.

Somewhere in the waves below she waited. The sun was exceptionally clear and warm, and he closed his eyes, reveling in its pleasing touch. After so many years, heaven was the birth of a new day. When he opened his eyes once more, he could feel them sparkle—sparkle with life and energy—sparkle with dreams. Below the Orca danced—timeless.

About the Author

David Niall Wilson is a USA Today bestselling, multiple Bram Stoker Award-winning author of more than forty novels and collections. He is a former president of the Horror Writers Association and CEO and founder of Crossroad Press Publishing. His novels include *This is My Blood, Deep Blue, Sins of the Flash,* and Many More. His most recent published works are the collection *The Devil's in the Flaws & Other Dark Truths,* the novella *When You Leave I Disappear, and t*he short novel *Closing Time at the Sunny Side Up,* available now from Shotgun Honey Press. David lives in way-out-yonder NC with his wife Patricia, 12 cats, and a chinchilla named Pook-Daddy.

Bibliography

HWA Bram Stoker Awards

2008: "The Gentle Brush of Wings" (*Defining Moments*) — short fiction — **winner**
2008: *Defining Moments* (Sarob Press) collection — **nomination**
2008: *Storytellers Unplugged* (by Joe Nassise & DNW) (Storytellers Unplugged) nonfiction — **nomination**
2004: *Roll Them Bones* (Cemetery Dance) — long fiction — **nomination**
2003: The Gossamer Eye (by Mark McLaughlin, Rain Graves & DNW) (Meisha Merlin) poetry collection — **winner**

Novels

This Is My Blood (1995)
Except You Go Through Shadow (1997)

The Temptation of Blood (2004)
Deep Blue (2004)
The Mote in Andrea's Eye (2006)
Ancient Eyes (2007)
Hallowed Ground (2011) with Steven Savile
Nevermore: A Novel of Love, Loss, & Edgar Allan Poe (2012)
Darkness Falling (2016)
On the Third Day (2016)
Remember Bowling Green: The Adventures of Frederick Douglass: Time Traveler (2017) with Patricia Lee Macomber
Gideon's Curse (2017)
Maelstrom (2019)
Jurassic Ark (2021)
Closing Time at the Sunny-Side-Up (2025)

The DeChance Chronicles

Heart of a Dragon (2013)
Vintage Soul (2009)
My Soul to Keep & Others - The Origin of Donovan DeChance (2011) [SF]
Kali's Tale (2012)
A Midnight Dreary (2018)

Tales of Old Mill, NC Featuring Cletus J. Diggs

The Not Quite Right Reverend Cletus J. Diggs & the Currently Accepted Habits of Nature (2011) [SF]
The Not Quite Right Reverend Cletus J. Diggs and the Crazy Case of Foreman James (2013)

O.C.L.T.

The Parting (2012)
The Temple of Camazotz (2011) [SF]
Crockatiel (2015) [Cletus J. Diggs crossover]

The Scattered Earth

The Second Veil (2011)

Star Trek: Universe

Voyager #12 - *Chrysalis* (1997) also appeared as:
Translation: *Puppen* [German] (1998)

Stargate Metaverse

Stargate Atlantis #15 *Brimstone* (2010) with Patricia Lee
Macomber

White Wolf World of Darkness

Dark Ages: Vampire

Dark Ages Clan Novel: *Lasombra* (2003)

The Grails Covenant Trilogy
To Sift Through Bitter Ashes (1997)
To Speak in Lifeless Tongues (1997)
To Dream of Dreamers Lost (1998)

Wraith

Except You Go Through Shadow (1997)

Exalted

Relic of the Dawn (2004)

Novellas

Roll Them Bones (2003)
The Preacher's Marsh (2008)
The Dun WHAT? Horror (2021) [Cletus J. Diggs DeChance
Chronicles crossover]
When You Leave I Disappear (2024)

Collections

The Fall of the House of Escher & Other Illusions (1996)
Defining Moments (2007)
Ennui and Other States of Madness (2008)
The Devil's in the Flaws & Other Dark Truths (2023)

Curious about other Crossroad Press books? Stop by our website: http://crossroadpress.com
We offer quality writing
in digital, audio, and print formats.

Subscribe to our newsletter on the website homepage and receive a free eBook.